HER TREASURED SEAL

MIDNIGHT DELTA SERIES, BOOK 10

CAITLYN O'LEARY

PASSIONATELY KIND PUBLISHING INC.

To all the men and women who serve.

SYNOPSIS

A Wedding. A Baby. But Will His Enemies Destroy Their Happiness?

Drake Avery has not gone out on a mission with his Navy SEAL team in months, instead he stayed by his woman's side as she fought for her life. Now Karen is home and recovering and it's time for Drake to go back to work. Joining his team to stop the Boko Haram in Africa, Drake faces his ultimate challenge.

Karen is happy to be home with her precious baby boy, but she soon discovers that planning a wedding with a newborn is a lot harder than she ever imagined. She's determined to be as strong as her man and hides how exhausted she is until it's almost too late.

As Karen and Drake attempt to fulfill their promise to honor, cherish, and love one another forever, powerful enemies have targeted them and the men of Midnight Delta. Will this couple ever get their happily ever after or will they be on the run for the rest of their lives?

1

"DRAKE, IT'S FINE."

Why the hell was Karen trying to reassure him, for fuck's sake? He kept what he hoped was a loving smile, plastered on his face as he brushed back her hair and kissed her forehead.

"Of course it's fine, Honey," he whispered.

"You'll feel just a little pressure, Karen," the doctor said from behind the draped area. Karen tried to hide her wince, but Drake spotted it.

"She's in pain," he roared.

"Drake," Karen gasped. "I'm okay."

"We're almost there," the doctor said.

A piercing wail startled Drake, yanking his gaze away from Karen. *What the hell?*

He pushed up from the wheeled stool and peered over the curtain where they had performed the Caesarean section on Karen. In Dr. Freeman's hands was a squalling red baby boy.

"Here's your healthy son, Mr. Avery." The doctor smiled up at him.

My God, had he ever seen anything more amazing in his life?

"Karen! Can you see him, Honey? Look up in the mirror." Drake grinned like a madman.

The wiggling, squalling scrap of life had him captivated. His son. He had a son. They had a son, my God, Karen was a miracle worker. "Listen to him, Karen, he's got a pair of lungs on him." He smiled broadly.

"Would you like to cut the cord?" Dr. Freeman asked.

In the excitement of the moment, he'd forgotten that part. He watched intently as they clamped off a section of the umbilical cord. A smiling nurse handed Drake a pair of scissors. Solemnly, he took them, and he looked at his son, who really was a bit of a mess, but he had that trademark Avery black hair, and God love him, he sure could yell.

Love swelled as he went to cut the cord, but then he hesitated.

"Will it hurt them?"

"No. Neither one of them will feel a thing." The doctor reassured him.

Like he was on a mission, he swiftly cut the cord. The crying stopped. He calmed. Almost as if he knew he was now part of a new world.

"Welcome home, Andrew," Drake whispered. A monitor started a shrill beeping behind him. It sounded worse than a fire drill on a ship.

What the fuck?

Drake's head whipped around. Karen was white as a sheet. Almost gray. Her eyes were closed.

He turned to ask the doctor what the hell was going on and saw the nurse beside Dr. Freeman whisk his son out of her arms. The doctor stood up and yanked back the drape that was separating Karen's head from her belly.

"What's her pressure?" the doctor demanded.

The nurse called it out.

"She's crashing, get Drake and the baby out of here," Dr. Freeman demanded.

"I'm not leaving," Drake said as he grabbed Karen's limp hand.

"Drake, I need you out of here," Dr. Freeman said firmly. "I need to take care of Karen. You're going to be in the way." Dr. Freeman leaned over Karen's stomach.

"Tell me what's going on. Now!" Drake was going out of his mind. Nothing could be wrong with Karen, he wasn't going to allow it. Not ever.

"Get him out of this room, now!" Dr. Freeman's entire demeanor changed, now she sounded like an admiral. Her tone brooked no argument.

"Karen's going to be fine, but you need to let Dr. Freeman do her job." A little nurse grabbed his arm and tugged him toward the door.

"I'm not leaving."

"You have to," she said firmly.

The door swung open and a man in scrubs rushed in. He barely spared Drake a glance except to say, "Leave. We need to attend to your wife."

All of Drake's focus was on Karen, the woman who by all rights was his wife, even though it still wasn't official.

"Please, Mr. Avery," the nurse pleaded. "Come with me. You're in the way. You're making things worse. You have to let them do their job."

He looked around the room. It was controlled chaos. The small woman tugged at him again. He walked out the door without any more trouble.

As soon as he was on the other side of the door, his fist hit the wall, going through plaster.

The nurse took three steps backward. *Fuck.*

"I won't hurt you," he said in a rough voice. It didn't seem to help. She turned and bustled down the hall. Probably to get security. He needed to...to...

He looked up, and there on the wall he saw a sign. *The* sign.

Drake strode down the hall where he had seen the stairs and took them three at a time to get to the second floor. Once he was in the chapel he hit his knees.

"God, it's me, Drake. I know we don't talk much, but don't hold that against Karen. Please don't, you can't, I'm begging you." He clasped his hands so tight they turned white.

"You made something perfect when you made her. She's in trouble." He gulped, trying to get his words just right, knowing he couldn't, then he just poured out his heart. "Please take me. I'm begging you, don't take her. I never deserved her. My life is nothing compared to hers." Drake didn't feel the tears on his cheeks as he bowed his head.

"Karen is precious. She shines. Our baby needs her. Please, don't take her. Let her live. I'll do anything, just let her live." He folded his arms against the bench in front of him and rested his head. "Let her live, take me," he chanted under his breath. "I'm begging you, let her live."

He was lost in his prayers, unaware of where he was, or how much time had passed, when a hand clamped down on his shoulder. He turned and saw his best friend. Before he could form a question, Mason provided an answer.

"It's all good," Mase said immediately. Drake slumped with relief.

He shut his eyes and whispered a word of thanks. Then scrubbed his face and got up.

"How'd you know where to find me?" Drake asked.

"It's where I'd be, if it was Sophia," Mason answered simply.

"Do you know what room she's in?" he demanded as they bolted toward the stairs.

"Five-fifteen," Mason answered. They made record time before crashing through the fifth-floor door. They received the evil eye of an orderly. Drake didn't give a shit. "Which way to room five-fifteen?" he demanded.

"Huh?"

He ran past the ignorant man and headed to the main nurse's station. "Room five-fifteen, where is it?" he demanded once again.

"Are you Drake Avery? We've been searching for you," a middle-aged woman answered. "Come with me. She's sleeping. Do you want to see your son?"

"I want to see Karen," he bit out. He'd seen his son. His son was healthy. He needed to see Karen more than he needed his next breath.

"This way."

He willed the woman to walk faster. Finally, she pointed to a room, he stopped himself from shoving her aside and slamming open the door, instead he gently pushed it open. His eyes zeroed in on Karen. She didn't have a breathing tube. That was a good sign, wasn't it? He rushed over to her, his hands hovering over her still form. He turned back to the nurse.

"What's wrong with her?"

"Nothing, now. She's sleeping off the anesthesia they gave her. The doctor said she should wake up in another hour."

"What happened to her? Is she going to be all right?"

"I'll get the doctor to come in and talk to you."

"Is she going to be all right?" Drake carefully enunciated each word in his most menacing tone.

"I'll be right back with Dr. Freeman." The nurse quickly left the room.

He turned to Mason. "Why wouldn't she answer me?"

"Steady. Your woman needs you to keep your shit together."

Drake took a deep breath. His friend, his lieutenant, was right. He sucked in a deep breath. When the door opened, and the doctor came in he didn't blast her. Especially since she was smiling.

"Drake. Karen's fine. She just had a little distress."

"What do you mean *little* distress, y'all were in emergency mode. You said she was crashing. She lost consciousness, the monitors were beeping. Don't tell me it was a little fucking distress." So much for keeping his shit together.

"Her blood pressure dropped significantly from the spinal anesthesia. We had to work fast to get it under control, otherwise there could have been...consequences."

Drake didn't want to think about the consequences. "But she's fine now?" he persisted.

"We got it under control. I can assure you, she's perfectly fine. This is only going to result in one extra day in the hospital. Maybe two."

"She's staying as long as she needs to! I don't want you sending her home before she's fully recovered from this trauma," Drake ordered.

Dr. Freeman gave him a mild smile. It was clear she was used to overbearing fathers.

"I'm serious," Drake growled.

"Drake?"

He spun around, all thought of Mason and Dr. Freeman

totally forgotten. "Karen! You're awake." He was on his knees beside her bed in an instant. He touched the fingers of her right hand. It was the best he could do, since her arms and hands were all connected to IVs, blood pressure cuffs, monitors and other things he didn't recognize.

"Drake, quit giving Dr. Freeman a hard time," Karen whispered weakly.

The doctor chuckled.

He touched his mouth to hers, wanting, no, needing that connection. His eyes remained opened as he assured himself she was alive and safe. Her fingers fluttered against his, he felt her try to move her hand, even though it should remain immobile. He pressed it down.

"I'm here, Honey," he said roughly, his voice choked with emotion. "Stay still."

"Where's our baby?"

"He's healthy. He's good." He turned to the doctor, who immediately stepped toward them.

"Your little boy is in the nursery. I'll have him brought in immediately." She smiled.

Karen's eyes drifted closed. "That's good. I want to see him," she said softly. Then she fell asleep.

"Is she okay?" Drake demanded.

"She's more than okay. She woke up sooner than expected. Your fiancée is a strong woman. She'll recover like a woman who had a normal C-Section, this is only going to add a day or two to her recovery. But like any woman who has undergone surgery she's going to need to take it easy when she gets home. Not just because of the C-Section, but because of all the time she spent on bedrest beforehand for the pre-eclampsia. It's going to take her awhile to get back up to speed."

"Trust me, she'll be wrapped in cotton wool."

He heard Mason cough behind him. He glared at his friend, knowing that was his way of saying he was going to have a hard time keeping Karen resting. Well, Mason could suck it. He would take care of his woman, even if he had to tie her to the bed.

"You don't need to go that far," the doctor smiled. "She'll recover at her own pace. Tomorrow, she'll need to get up and moving."

"Only if she feels like it," Drake qualified.

"No, you don't understand, moving around is necessary for her recovery," the doctor countered. "I'll be back in an hour." She left.

"We're going to go get some dinner. Text us when we can come back and visit Karen and the baby," Mason said as he headed toward the door.

"Mase." Drake stopped him.

"Yeah?"

"Before we're surrounded by people, Karen and I wanted to tell you something. Since she's asleep, I guess it's up to me."

Mason gave him a quizzical glance.

"We decided to name the little guy Andrew Mason Avery."

Drake saw his words sink in. Mason's eyes said everything worth saying. Drake understood all that Mason couldn't say. How could he not? They were brothers of the heart.

"I'm honored, Drake."

"You damn well should be." Drake grinned, lightning the moment.

Mason barked out a laugh, then immediately stopped, looking at Karen.

Drake peered over at her as well, she was still out like a

light. "I'll text you when she and Andrew are ready for visitors. Thank everybody for hanging around. Are Jack and Beth still cool with picking up Karen's mom from the airport?"

"Do you really have to ask?"

"That was a stupid question," Drake agreed. His teammates always had his six. Karen's water had broken late last night, a week sooner than the planned C-Section, which is why Karen's mom wasn't here from Alaska.

Andrew.

Andrew Mason Avery.

His son.

Drake stared down at the small scrap of humanity in his arms. He looked at his exhausted woman lying in the hospital bed. Had she ever looked more beautiful? Antsy, he stood up holding his small son. He knelt beside the bed and placed the baby next to Karen, wrapping his arms around the two most precious people in his world. He kissed the top of her head, willing her to wake up.

Karen surfaced in a whirl of confusion, until finally she zeroed in on one thought.

Andrew.

Andrew Mason Avery.

She had a son.

Her eyes snapped open. Where was her baby? It hurt to move. She carefully rolled her head on the pillow and saw two dark heads beside her. She desperately wanted to touch the delicate lips of her son. She wanted to make sure he was breathing. If not that, then she wanted to place her palm against his chest and feel the flutter of his heartbeat. Unfortunately, she found both of her arms were bound to her sides, connected to wires and tubes. Her eyes filled with tears of frustration.

"Karen, what's wrong?" Drake asked quietly. His chocolate brown eyes were filled with love and concern.

"I can't even lift my arms to touch Andrew," she whimpered softly. She hated that she felt tears coming on, but the fact that she couldn't touch her own baby was breaking her heart.

"Shhhh, Honey, I've got your back." Drake gently picked up the sleeping baby and moved him down next to her hand. She lifted her fingers and stroked his downy cheek.

"He's so soft," she marveled. Then she pressed her fingers against his small bow mouth like she'd wanted to, and she felt a tiny puff of air. She sighed with contentment. "He's perfect, Drake. Look at that head of hair. He looks like you."

"He has your eyes," Drake said softly.

"Are you sure? Most babies have blue eyes, maybe they just look green."

Drake raised an eyebrow and gave her an amused glance.

"You wouldn't have made a mistake." She laughed. Then she winced.

"Dammit, you're in pain. I need to call the doctor, or the nurse."

"It was nothing. Just a twinge."

"Bullshit. You never complain."

Karen laughed and winced again. "What are you talking

about? I complained all the way to the hospital. Labor pains *hurt*."

"I don't know whose truck you were in, but you weren't in mine. My God woman, you would occasionally let out a squeak or moan, but you didn't bitch once. I remember begging you to scream. Anything to let loose. But you wouldn't, you just bore the pain like a warrior princess."

"Some warrior princess. As soon as we got to the operating room, I was asking for drugs."

"You're not remembering things clearly, I was demanding drugs *for* you."

Karen smiled. She did remember Drake's roars. It was one of the few times people didn't jump when he demanded things. Apparently, the staff was used to distraught fathers.

"Karen, you scared the hell out of me." Drake brushed back her hair and kissed her forehead. Tears formed in her eyes. "You're my everything, Karen. I don't know what I would do without you."

"I'm here, and I'm okay."

"You weren't. You crashed. They shoved me out of the room, so they could work on you. Karen, I almost lost you." She saw the wet in his eyes. Once again, she was frustrated that she couldn't move her arms.

"Honey, I'm here. Everything's okay."

"Andrew is going to be an only child."

She stared at him. They'd been talking about a big family since the day they decided to get married. He couldn't be serious.

As if he read her mind, he said, "I'm serious. There is no fucking way on this Earth that I'm going to risk your life again. Don't even think about changing my mind."

The tiny bundle in Drake's arms squirmed. Karen's focus shifted from her man's fierce gaze to her son. She watched in fascination as Andrew's eyes opened slightly, his little fist punching out.

"I don't think he likes you swearing, Drake," she tried to joke.

"The nurse said he'd be hungry pretty soon."

Karen looked down at her arms again and once again her eyes filled with tears.

"Hey...hey...Let me call the nurse. You need something for the pain anyway." Drake Andrew and headed for the door.

"I'm not in pain," she called out loudly. Ouch, that hurt. She needed to keep her voice down. No laughing either. Drake didn't miss her flinch.

"Drugs. You're getting drugs."

"Drugs are bad for the baby," she said.

"We'll see."

He was out the door before she had a chance to say anything further.

The next thing she knew he was back with a nurse.

"Let's get you situated, shall we?" the nurse said. She came over to Karen and unhooked some of the monitors from her right arm, and attached them to her left. Her IV was already hooked up to her left so that wasn't a problem. "There you go, you're all set. I'm also going to give you something for the pain."

"I don't want anything that will harm Andrew."

"What a great name," the nurse smiled. "I promise, this won't hurt the little guy while you're nursing. You being in pain is something that won't help either of you. You need to take it easy and recover."

"I told you." Drake smirked.

"I'm going to stay with you for a few minutes while you get the hang of nursing, all right?"

Karen was both embarrassed and relieved. The nurse caught on immediately, but Drake didn't.

"What's there to get the hang of?" he asked. "Isn't it just suck and go?"

"Actually, it's not. A lot of the bigger hospitals have a lactation specialist who will help mothers 'learn the art' of nursing," she said using her fingers as quotation marks.

Karen laughed. "I swear I've read every baby book I could get my hands on, but I sure would appreciate it if you could watch a few minutes to tell me if I'm doing it right. What's your name?"

"I'm Alice. And I know you're Karen, and this little guy's name is Andrew, but who's the big fella?"

Drake held out his hand. "I'm Drake." He smiled. "I'm interested in learning the art of nursing."

"Most men are."

Karen laughed. "I just want to make sure that Andrew gets all the nourishment he needs. Also, I hear that he might get too much air. Or that he might not want to nurse, or even that—"

"You're going to be a natural." Drake and Alice said almost in unison.

"Seriously Karen, it's going to be fine."

And it was. Soon Andrew was feeding like a Rockstar, and Alice left them alone.

She and Drake looked down at their son feeding from her breast, then back into one another's eyes. The intimacy of the moment was breathtaking. Andrew's little fist pressed against her. She sighed contentedly as he suckled.

"He sure knows what he wants." Drake smiled.

"He's his daddy's boy."

"He better not tire you out."

Karen giggled. That was exactly what babies did, tired

their mothers out. What was Drake thinking? Andrew batted his hand against her breast in protest at her movement. She bit her lip to keep from laughing again.

"He doesn't like it when you mess with his food supply," Drake murmured. He touched Andrew's cheek with his finger. His finger looked huge against the infant. Drake's hand could easily encompass their baby's whole head.

"He's tiny," Drake said what she was thinking.

"I wonder what he weighs."

"He's eight pounds, seven ounces."

How did he know that? She wanted to ask how long she'd been unconscious, but she knew bringing that up would just poke the tiger, so she kept her mouth shut. "Eight and a half pounds is big, Drake."

"He still looks tiny to me."

"I hate to be the one to tell you this," she whispered. "But you're kind of on the large side."

He let out a laugh. Once again, Andrew showed his displeasure by batting his hand against her breast. They both looked at their son with wonder. There wasn't a chance in hell they were only going to have an only child. Even if they had to adopt, they were going to have a houseful, Karen vowed to herself.

Finally, Andrew started to lose steam. Drake picked up their tired son in one hand.

"You look good holding Andrew. You do it so easily."

"I should. I might not remember carrying Trenda around, but I was holding Evie when I was probably four years old. I was feeding and diapering Maddie when I was seven, and Trenda and I practically raised the twins and Piper."

Karen winced thinking about Drake being no more than a baby himself taking care of other babies. Dammit, he needed someone in his corner, fighting the good fight with him. Karen yawned.

"How can I be this tired?" she asked.

"Are you seriously asking that?" He gently set their boy down in the bassinette beside her bed. He came back and touched his lips to hers in a warm, sweet kiss. With tender care, he pulled up her gown and put it back into place, then covered her with the blanket. "Sleep, Honey," he whispered.

"Not tired. Just need to rest my eyes for a moment," she said right before she fell asleep.

2

AN HOUR AND A HALF LATER, DRAKE GOT A TEXT FROM JACK that he was headed back with Wilma Eastman. Drake looked over at Karen and saw that she was still resting her eyes. He looked down at Andrew who was staring back at him. He loved it. He hadn't expected a newborn to have his eyes open. The nurse had told him that he couldn't really focus on Drake, but he knew better. They were bonding at a soul level.

"Drake?" He turned his head and saw that Karen was awake. How long had he been staring at Andrew? He put the baby in his bassinette and knelt beside Karen.

"You're going to hurt your knees," she warned.

"I don't think hospital linoleum is going to injure me." He held her hand and slid his cheek against hers. Her skin was as soft as their son's. Their lips met. He would never take her for granted, she was his world. Karen and Andrew.

"Where is everyone?" Karen asked.

"Your mother should be here in less than thirty minutes. The Avery Avalanche has been waiting less than patiently outside. I told them you needed some time to recover."

"But they've seen Andrew, right?"

"Nope. I told them that you would show him off." When he saw her glowing smile, he knew he'd made the right decision. "The team is here too. All of them but Trenda and Bella went out to dinner a couple of hours ago, but they've been back for a while. If I had to guess, Sophia has been feeding them all baked goods in the waiting room."

"Do you think she smuggled in any for me?"

"I'm sure she did, but you, Warrior Princess, are on strict orders to do whatever the doc says. If she says you can have smuggled baked goods, then fine. If she doesn't, then you don't."

"You're bossy, do you know that?"

"I'm second-in-command. I'm paid to be bossy."

Karen made a small move to sit up, and gasped. "What the fuck?" he demanded as he pushed her softly back toward the pillow. "What in the hell are you trying to do?"

"Greet visitors of course. Granted, I went about it the wrong way. Can you help me sit up?"

Drake found the button to raise the bed. "Tell me if this gets to be uncomfortable." He watched her like a hawk, making sure that she wasn't enduring unnecessary pain. Satisfied that the bed was in enough of an upright position, and that she hadn't made any painful facial expressions, he stopped pressing the button. She blew out a deep breath through her teeth.

"Enough of this shit," he decreed. He stood up and pressed the button for the nurse. "It's time for more pain meds."

"That might not be a bad idea," Karen agreed.

He leaned close, making sure she wouldn't miss a word. "You scare me, you hide pain the way one of my SEAL teammates would. You're not on a mission. You're a new mother, and I'm here to help you. You did the same thing when you were hurt back in Tennessee, I told you then that it was bullshit. Lean on me, Karen. In a little over a month I'm going to be your husband."

"You're my husband now, in every way that matters," she said as she lifted her hand and cupped his cheek. Her thumb brushed over his bottom lip and he shuddered.

"My God woman, you never fail to arouse me."

Her eyes searched his. "Are you sure? I haven't felt like me for so long, and now I'm a real mess."

"You're Karen. You're always going to do it for me. Even when we're both in our rocking chairs, one look from your sparkling green eyes and I'm going to be chasing you into the bedroom or into the kitchen if that's closer." He spoke nothing but the truth and he was satisfied to see her apprehension melt away.

"Bring Andrew here, I want to love on him again."

Drake smiled. He brought their boy to Karen. "I was wrong, he is tiny," she said. "Look at the nails on his fingers, they are miniscule. But look at that head of hair. It's just like yours, Drake." He looked at the awe on her face, then he looked down at their baby. His heart clutched.

"I still can't believe we made him." Drake stroked his tiny hand.

"Unwrap him," Karen said. "I want to see his feet."

Drake grinned. He'd already counted Andrew's toes, and kissed the bottom of his feet. Something told him Karen was about to do the same thing.

"Oh look, his feet are big, he's going to wear your size shoe." She grinned up at him.

"What the hell are you talking about? His feet are as small as his hands." Okay, maybe not that little, but still, put the kid down next to his boot and he'd bet the farm they were the same size.

"He's going to grow up huge, just like his Daddy." Karen kissed Andrew's cheek, and then reached up and kissed Drake's. "Thank you for giving me this miracle."

"I can't believe we did this. How did we do this Karen? Does every parent feel like this? I want to protect him and not let anything bad ever happen to him, but at the same time I want to help him conquer the world, ya know? How can I ever do this right?"

"What are you talking about?" she gently admonished. "I should be the one who's worried. You already raised some amazing women, I was the youngest sibling."

He looked at her in amazement. "Are you kidding? Piper told me how you had your class of kindergartners eating out of your hand. With your heart and brains, you're going to be the best mother in the world. Do you want to know a secret?"

She looked up at him, hanging onto every word. She nodded.

"Even if I weren't head over heels in love with you, I would still choose you to be the mother of my child. You were meant to do this."

"I hope I can live up to your belief in me." She kissed the bottom of Andrew's foot, then swaddled him back up in his blanket.

"There is not a doubt in my mind Baby, not one single doubt."

His phone buzzed, and he saw that it was Jack.

"Jack says they're still fifteen minutes away. Do you want to wait for your mom?"

"Nope, she gets here when she gets here. I don't want to keep the others waiting any longer. Call them in."

The door opened, and Alice came in. "I brought another pain pill," she said cheerfully. "Oh good, you're sitting up. Tomorrow we'll see about getting you out of bed."

"You can't be serious," Drake turned around to stare at her.

"Just a walk to the bathroom and back. The day after that we'll have her walk to the nurse's station. She needs to get up and move." She handed Karen the pill and watched as she swallowed it with a sip of water. "You were on bedrest for a long while, weren't you?"

"Yes," Karen answered.

"We need to get you back in fighting form, so you can take care of baby Andrew."

"I'll take care of him. Karen needs to recover. Maybe we should postpone the wedding."

The atmosphere in the room went still.

He wanted to kick his own ass when he saw the look of dismay on Karen's face. Even Alice gave him a sharp look.

"I wasn't thinking, of course we won't delay the wedding, Honey." He needed to backpedal fast. "Karen, I didn't mean it. I just want you to take all the time you need to recover, is all." His Tennessee accent came out thicker as he tried to talk himself out of the hole he'd dug.

She didn't answer him, just stared. Fuck, he needed to do damage control, STAT. He took the glass of water from Karen and leaned in next to her. "If we could, I'd bring in a priest, a minister, or a judge, and marry you in this hospital room right this moment."

She stared at him like he had lost his mind.

"Karen, making sure you're healthy is the most important thing in my world. If trying to schedule and have a big wedding is too much for you, then I want to postpone it." He saw her consider his words. "So do I call a minister? Everybody's outside, we could get it done now."

"Drake Jefferson Avery, we are not getting married on the day I gave birth," she said in a deadly calm voice. Oh shit, he was really in trouble. "We are getting married in seven weeks like we planned. Like Alice just said I am going to get up and walk, I am going to recover, and we are not changing our effing plans, am I being perfectly clear? Even for you?"

He bit the inside of his cheek. "Yes ma'am. Message received."

"Good, now I need to see our friends," she said crisply. "I want to show off our son."

So did he. Everybody out in that waiting room was family. He needed to share this day with them.

He feathered a kiss against his woman's forehead and gently placed her back against the pillows, then he took out his cell phone and texted his oldest sister. She pinged him back in a nanosecond. Next, he texted Mason who was even quicker in his response, as if that were possible.

"I think our family is going to be descending. You ready?"

"More than."

Their son was cuddled close to his mama just a moment before a soft knock sounded on the door. Drake opened it and found Trenda holding her young daughter Bella, with Mason, Sophia, and her sixteen-year-old brother Billy, standing behind her. He looked behind them expecting more people.

"They were stopped at the nurse's station. Clint is doing a song and dance to allow more people to come in at the same time. The hoard should be in soon," Mason explained all this as Trenda scooted in past Drake. As if his words magically conjured his family, Drake saw his five other sisters coming down the hall with Evie and Chloe's husbands Zarek and Aiden.

Drake grinned at Mason as he saw them, and Sophia and Billy slid by him into the room. "I see the Avery Avalanche." Mason looked over his shoulder and gave his fellow SEAL, Aiden, a chin tilt. Aiden gave a small smile in return, happy that his wife, Evie, was so thrilled to see her nephew.

"Hurry," Evie and Piper said at the same moment as they both tugged at Aiden's hands. Aiden broke into a grin and hurried. Drake was about bowled over when his sister Maddie plowed into him.

"You broke the curse. A son! I'm so happy for you, Big Brother." She was crying through her smile. "I love you Drake, now get out of the way." Drake looked over his shoulder and saw that Sophia was holding Bella and Trenda was holding Andrew. Maddie went straight to the sink to wash her hands, intuitively knowing the drill.

Drake was hugged by Evie, Chloe, Zoe, and Piper and then abandoned as they rushed into the room. Zarek, Chloe's husband, shook his hand and congratulated him before going into room, that left Aiden.

"Where's everybody else?" Drake asked.

"Clint managed to sweet talk the nurse into letting your overabundant clan in. I think he and Dare are planning an op up the back stairs to get the SEAL team in here in the next few minutes."

They grinned at one another. "I'm amazed that Finn hasn't acquired hospital attire for everyone," Drake said.

"That has been discussed. I think that's the back-up plan."

God, he loved his team.

"Get your ass in here, and see my boy."

"By the way, great name," Aiden said as he clapped him on the back and went to join Evie. Drake zeroed in on Karen, making sure that she was doing okay. Now instead of pale, she looked flushed. Drake frowned. Was it a good flushed, or bad flushed? He went over to the side of the bed near the wall and rested his hand on her shoulder so that he could brush his knuckles against her cheek. She felt hot.

"Drake, I'm fine," she said smiling up at him. Damn, he couldn't slip anything past her.

"I want to hug Auntie Karen," Bella said. She tugged at the blanket covering Karen, who winced. Drake opened his mouth, but before he had a chance to say anything, Zoe swung her niece up in her arms and started tickling her.

"We need to be gentle with Auntie Karen, Lovebug. Her tummy is sore."

"Can I kiss her?"

Zoe aimed Bella at Karen. "Kisses!" Bella shouted, then smacked Karen a wet one before Zoe pulled her back. "Mommy, I want a brother, like baby Andrew."

Trenda, who was still holding onto her nephew, with her four other sisters crowded around her, looked up at her daughter. "You'll have to make do with your cousin for the time being, Bella." Drake noted the wistful look on his oldest sister's face. Talk about a woman who should have a houseful of children.

"My turn," Evie said holding out her hands. Trenda reluctantly gave up Andrew and transferred him to her sister. Evie then turned around and looked at Mason. "I think it's time for you to hold your namesake."

Mason's eyes warmed as he took Andrew from Evie. God, the kid looked miniscule when he went from pint-sized Evie to warrior-sized Mason Gault. Mason's wife

Sophia leaned in, and both of them stared intently at Andrew. It was as if they were ensconced in a world of their own. Andrew got his fist free from his blue blanket and curled it around Mason's pinkie. Drake watched as tears spilled down Sophia's cheeks. She turned to him and Karen, and mouthed, "Thank you," then turned back to the baby.

The door opened and in walked his fellow SEAL team members and their women. First came Clint and his fiancée Lydia, then Angie and Finn, and finally Dare and his wife Rylie. After receiving three chin tilts he watched as the women gathered with his sisters and the men went to the window to join Aiden and Zarek, it was as if there was a magical bubble that surrounded Mason, Sophia and Andrew for the moment. Drake knew that they had been struggling to have children, so this moment was even more precious. Dammit, they were meant to be parents. Even though Billy was part of their family, he stood aside, giving the couple their time, his expression empathetic.

"When can I play with my dozen?" Bella asked in a loud whisper. Everybody laughed, and Andrew let out a soft cry. The poignant moment was over.

"Cousin, Honey. Andrew is your cousin," Trenda said, emphasizing the 'C'.

"Can I hold my Zuzin?" she asked. Sophia and Mason turned and smiled at the little girl.

"If she sits in my lap, can we hold Andrew together?" Trenda asked Drake and Karen.

"Of course," Karen answered.

At least ten cell phones were whipped out to take pictures. "Drake, take a picture," Karen exclaimed.

"We'll have forty-seven texted to us. We're good. I like it where I am." He stroked her beautiful auburn hair. There wasn't a chance in hell he was going to leave her side unless he was dragged away. He listened as his four-year-old niece continued to butcher the word cousin. God, she was a doll. Too bad she lived in Tennessee, otherwise she could babysit Andrew one day.

The door opened again, and in walked an older version of Karen, flanked by Drake's team mate, Jack Preston and his wife Beth. Wilma Eastman took in the scene, smiled at her grandson, and made a beeline to her daughter's bed.

"You look flushed. Jack and Beth said there were complications." She immediately glared at Drake, as if he were at fault.

"Mom, I'm fine," Karen attempted to soothe.

"Drake, tell me everything. Karen's just going to lie. Is my baby girl all right? What happened?"

Drake sure as shit wasn't going to tell Karen's mom everything. Especially with Karen trying to grind his knuckles together. He knew she would never forgive him. Plus, he agreed. What was the point in going over things that were in the past? Hell, the only reason to ever inform Karen that a mission went a little sideways is if he came home with a new scar. And even then, he downplayed the hell out of it.

"The doctor said she's going to be fine, Wilma. But, because of all the bedrest she's had, we're going to wait on her hand and foot for a good long while until she's recovered."

Karen shifted to glare at him and then she let out an *eep* of pain. Both Wilma and Drake zeroed in on her. "Honey, don't strain yourself," Wilma soothed.

"Karen," Drake gave a low warning whisper.

"Both of you stop. I'll be out of here in four days." Karen rolled her head toward her Mom, then back the other way so she had Drake in her sites. "I'm going to be up out of this bed walking the halls the day after tomorrow. I am not made out of spun glass."

"Honey, I didn't say you were spun glass-" he started.

"You are not waiting on me hand and foot. I want to take care of my baby. You're not taking away one single moment of mine and Andrew's time together; do you hear me?"

Wilma started chuckling, and the sound of female laughter filled the room. "You tell him, Sister," Evie chimed in. "Are you listening, Aiden? None of this cotton wool shit is going to fly."

"Auntie Evie, you said a bad word, you owe me money," Bella said.

"Dammit."

"Two dollars pease." Bella grinned triumphantly. Male chuckles interspersed with the female giggles. Trenda made sure she had a steady hold on Andrew as Bella jumped out of the chair to hit up her aunt for cash.

"Welcome to the crazy." Drake smiled at Wilma.

"I had four kids. I've been dying for grandchildren to add to the mayhem." She kissed Karen's forehead and stroked her cheek. "Shouldn't you be sleeping?"

"I wouldn't miss this for the world." Then she yawned. "But if I do fall asleep, there will be enough pictures to last a lifetime." Drake noted all the phones that were out and poised to take more shots, and knew she was right.

Drake saw Wilma take her fourth glance over at Andrew, and Trenda must have seen her doing it too, because she brought him over. "Here, Grandma, someone needs a cuddle."

Andrew let out a cry, and Wilma laughed. She immediately started to walk with him, rocking and cooing. Andrew settled. When Drake looked back at Karen he saw she was asleep, despite the fact there were over fifteen people in her room. Trenda and Mason were soon at his side.

"We're going to gather the troops and head out," Mason said.

"We'll be back tomorrow." Trenda smiled.

He watched as his sister and lieutenant herded everyone out of the room.

"Jack is going to drop me off at your apartment. I'm staying in Piper's room, while she stays at Evie's with the rest of your sisters." She handed off Andrew and kissed Drake on his cheek. "I'll have something warming in the oven when you get home."

"I'm going to sleep in the chair tonight." Drake nodded at the recliner in the corner.

"Are you sure?"

"Yep. I want to stay close. Thanks for coming, Wilma."

"Are you going to tell me what happened?" she asked, looking him dead in the eye.

"Nope."

She sighed. "I'll see you tomorrow morning. Think about what I said during our last telephone conversation. It sure would be nice."

"Wilma, you being Karen's mom means I love you. Don't doubt it. The word mom leaves a bitter taste in my mouth. Now the name Wilma makes me smile." Holding Andrew in one arm, he wrapped his other around her shoulder as he walked her to the door where Jack and Beth were waiting.

3

"MOM, DRAKE'S DRIVING ME INSANE. HE NEEDS TO GO BACK to base."

Her mother laughed as she tossed the clean clothes on the bed and started to fold them. Karen carefully picked up Andrew in a sideways hold, so she didn't abuse her tummy too much. Little Man wiggled and kicked her in the side with his foot. She caught his toe and tickled it. To her mind, her son could do no wrong, even if he did cause his Mama a little extra pain.

"Sweetie, you need to relax. You're trying to push things. That's why Drake's bothering you so much."

"I have to push things. I'm getting married in five-and-a-half weeks."

"All the more reason for Drake to be here so you can lean on him."

Not for the wedding she wasn't. She'd told him months ago that she had this under control, she wasn't going to admit now that it had all blown up in her face. How could months of careful planning backfire so badly? First the caterer goes out of business, and then the band she'd hired breaks up. It was like she was cursed.

"Drake's pitching in a lot Mom. He's wonderful with Andrew, he's up at all hours, I couldn't ask for anything more."

"Then what are you stewing about?" her mom asked as she efficiently folded clothes and started to put them away in the dresser.

"Nothing."

"I call bullshit."

Karen grinned at her mother, but before she was forced to answer, her cell phone rang. Saved by the bell. It was one of the caterers on Catalina Island she had reached out to. The one she had originally arranged to cater the wedding had gone out of business. She was frantically trying to find one who could fit her in, and wouldn't cost too much since she had lost a deposit. Thank God Sophia was arranging for all the desserts. Could she just serve dessert for the wedding?

As soon as she got off the phone she saw her mother's expression and went to give her a hug.

"Your dad is just heartbroken about this. So am I for that matter."

"Oh my God, Mom, you need to stop. Drake and I were never going to allow you to pay for the wedding even if you tried to. It was our decision to do this. We're doing it on a budget because we're saving for a townhome near Clint and Lydia. Between selling my home in Tennessee and Drake's savings we have down payment, enough for savings and a wedding. It's just we want to start a college fund for Andrew, so we're keeping to a budget."

"Don't kid a kidder. This is California, I've looked up the home prices out here."

"That's why we're getting a townhome."

"And a wedding?"

"We're getting a deal on the venue. One of Drake's buddies from another SEAL team has an old girlfriend who got us an outrageously low price, that's why we could afford to have it on Catalina Island." Karen had to pause. Every time she thought about the view they had she wanted to cry. It was going to be gorgeous. The wedding was going to take place on the secluded side of the island called Two Harbors. There was a lodge that they had rented out for the entire wedding party and some of the guests. They were getting married in a meadow, and the reception was going to take place next to some Live Oak trees that butted up to a cliff overlooking the ocean. It couldn't get any prettier.

"Still, we always wanted to give you the wedding of your dreams."

"Mom, you needed the money for medical bills. You and Dad need to stop obsessing. I'm just grateful you didn't lose the house. What's more, I *am* getting the wedding of my dreams."

"What did this new caterer say?" her mother asked, changing the subject.

Karen let out a dejected sigh. "They can't do it on such short notice. But they were nice enough to send out an SOS to some of the other people on the island that they thought might be able to help. She warned me that at least two of the outfits that she contacted were really new though, and she couldn't give a first-hand recommendation."

"That was nice of her to be so up front."

"Mom, I don't know what I'm going to do if this doesn't work." Karen's stomach churned and she actually felt like crying. Damned hormones. Then she heard the front door of the apartment open. She needed to get it together before

Drake saw her so upset. The last thing she needed was him coddling her even more.

"I'm going to go help him put away the groceries. I don't want you to worry, it will all work out, Sweetheart." As soon as her mother left the room, Andrew let his presence be known by letting out a wail.

"I'm sorry, Baby Boy, was Mommy not paying attention to you?" Karen placed Andrew into his infant seat, so he could sit up a little bit. She swore that even at one and a half weeks he liked to look around. According to the baby books that wasn't true, but his head turned in her direction when she moved around the room.

She knelt down and stared at him. His hair had already started to get thicker.

"When is Mommy going to have to get you a haircut? Huh?" He huffed out a sigh. "What, no haircut? Okay. I can cope with that." She touched the silky black strands. Andrew's arms waved and knocked into her. "You're a strong little boy, aren't you?"

Andrew blew a bubble and looked at her. She placed a kiss against his warm cheek. Just being around him settled her. To hell with the caterers. But then her cell phone rang, and it was one of the newly suggested caterers who said they couldn't do the job, and her stomach began to churn again.

Andrew started crying. She looked at the clock on the dresser and realized it was time for his lunch.

"Honey, you okay?" Drake carefully pulled her into his arms from behind. His warmth and gentleness brought tears to her eyes. She blinked them back. For God's sake, when would she stop being so emotional?

"Karen?" Drake turned her around, so he could look at her.

"Andrew," she protested, her hand waving at their

crying son.

"He can wait. Tell me what's wrong."

"Nothing. You're being too nice." She smashed her face into his chest and breathed in his scent. It soothed her. *He* soothed her.

"Being nice to you is my job."

"Drake, you're in the Navy. That's your job. You've been babysitting me for months." His hand stopped mid-stroke, then he resumed.

"I'm still in the Navy. I'm on family leave. It has us covered."

She felt the hesitation.

"How many missions have you missed?"

"I don't know."

"Liar."

"I've been exactly where I needed to be." Andrew cried louder, and Karen pulled out of Drake's arms.

"Bubba needs his feeding," Karen said, not looking up at Drake.

"I vote against that nickname for my boy."

"Okay, Love." Karen thought about Drake's villainous family tree back in Tennessee, she didn't know of a specific Bubba, but maybe there was one. She bent wrong to pick up Andrew. She thought she hid her wince, but Drake caught it. He picked up the infant seat from the bed and put it on the floor, then he swooped her in his arms and had her on the bed and resting against the pillows before she could say a word of protest.

"I thought we agreed your mom and I would do all the heavy lifting."

"Well you're sure doing that," Karen muttered.

Drake's head shot up as he picked up a crying Andrew. "Are you picking on my woman's luscious curves?"

Karen looked down at her flabby belly. Luscious her fat ass.

"Karen, look at me."

Karen continued to stare down at her abdomen.

"Honey, how many hours of sleep are you getting each day? Are you napping like you should?" She thought about how often the phone rang. "Answer me."

"You're here, you know I lie down."

"Yes, but you're not sleeping, are you?" He went over to the nightstand and pulled the two bottles of medicine that the doctor had prescribed. One was an over-the-counter pain reliever the other was something stronger. He opened them both up. "Dammit woman, you're not even taking your medicine according to the recommended dosage."

"I want to stay alert for Andrew." And figure out the wedding stuff.

"I'm here, you rest, I'll be alert for Andrew, problem solved."

She bit her lip, because that really didn't solve the wedding issue. She really did need her wits about her.

Drake's eyes got wide, then they narrowed. "You're now on lockdown."

"What?"

"You need your sleep. Your mother and I are here to take care of Andrew. You need to take care of yourself so that you're not in pain, so you can recover faster. Choosing not to take your medicine is not helping. You can't sleep because you're in pain, right?"

"For God's sake Drake, women have babies every second of every day. This is not a big deal. Hell, most of them do it without going to the hospital. I certainly don't need a pill because I have an owie."

He glared at her. "Most women aren't on mandatory

bedrest for damn near five months before they give birth because their health is in danger. Most women don't almost die from giving birth. Most women aren't *my* woman. You will take care of yourself, do you hear me?"

She swallowed. He looked fierce, but beneath that she could see that he was actually the one in pain.

"I hear you," she said quietly.

He tossed the pill bottles back in the drawer, and cradled Andrew over his shoulder. Then he rested one knee on the bed and stroked a finger down the side of her jaw. "Look at me, Honey. You're hurting right now, aren't you?"

Damn the man was smart. He played at being a goof, but he was smart as hell. Karen nodded. He left the room, jostling their son so he hiccupped instead of wailed. He was good with their boy too. Drake came back with a glass of water. "You're going to take a pill, then feed Andrew, then I'm going to hold you while you go to sleep, does that sound good?"

It sounded wonderful too bad it didn't work. She fell asleep, but only for a moment and when she woke, Drake's breathing was soft and even. That's what always happened, she'd sleep for twenty minutes then wake up with her mind racing. She'd had a whole different idea of what it would be like after she'd given birth. She'd be up and around and not depending on anyone, least of all Drake. After five months of him waiting on her hand and foot because of the bedrest, she'd been bound and determined to stand on her own two feet. Drake had spent all of his damned life taking care of others. What was even more horrific was that his parents had beaten him down. Not once had someone taken care of him. She had promised herself that she would be that person for him, and she was failing. Not just because of the wedding, but because he felt the need to stay home from missions. She knew her man, she knew it was killing him. Some how, some way, she had to convince him that she was okay on her own. That she could handle things. She needed to man up. She didn't want to be one more weight that Drake had to carry.

She could do this. She knew she was capable. Hell, she'd moved across the country, left her family behind to start a new life for herself. She could handle this. Yep, she would be someone that Drake could rely on.

And on that note, Karen closed her eyes, and prayed she would sleep for a while.

DRAKE PUT his son in his bassinette, and tucked an afghan around his sleeping wife. He'd stopped mentally correcting himself months ago. Karen was his wife, and would have been six months ago if she hadn't had this idiotic idea about having a Christmas wedding after their baby was born. He took one last look at his little family before leaving the room.

As he walked by Piper's room, he heard Wilma on the phone with someone. As much as he loved having his soon-to-be mother-in-law here to help Karen, he missed his baby sister. He pulled out his cell phone and called the real estate agent. He got her voice mail.

"Avery, here. Roberta, can you get back to me about the townhome I told you about this morning? I want to know if we can see it and put a bid on it before it goes on the market."

Clint Archer, the team's computer tech, had been keeping an eye out for townhomes in and around his complex. He'd called to tell him one was going on the market tomorrow, and he needed to act fast. Drake suspected that Clint had somehow delayed the listing from appearing online, so Drake could get a jump on it, but when he pushed his friend, Clint denied it. Drake wasn't buying it.

After he hung up he scrolled through the texts that had come in while he'd held Karen. Shit, one of the texts was from Mason and it was marked urgent. He should have checked them before calling Roberta.

"Can you come to base?" Mason asked before Drake even had a chance to say a word.

Drake knew it was important, or his lieutenant wouldn't be asking. "I'm leaving in less than five."

"Preciate it." The phone went dead.

Drake went down the hall and knocked on the halfway open bedroom door where Wilma was sitting on the bed and staring out the window.

"You okay?" they asked simultaneously.

Drake answered first. "I have to head to the base. Do you have things covered? Andrew and Karen are sleeping."

Wilma gave a perky smile. "You go on. What would you like for dinner?"

Something was wrong. Wilma was always upbeat, but there was something off with 'perky'. He didn't have time to probe. He'd get to the bottom of it when he got home.

"Anything you cook will be great. I'll be back as soon as I can."

He left the apartment, got in his truck and headed for the base at Coronado.

———

"CLOSE THE DOOR," Mason said as Drake walked into his office. Mason looked tense. Suddenly, Drake felt like he did when he had been put before a judge to decide to either go into the Navy or serve time. What the hell was going on? Mason looked up from the file on his desk.

"Jesus, Drake, this isn't about you. I'm sorry, Man, I'm handling this all wrong."

Drake relaxed. "This has to be a personnel issue, or you wouldn't be so twisted. It's got to be one of us."

"It's Finn."

Fuck. Finn Crandall had struggled with PTSD last year. He'd gone undercover on a human trafficking ring with young women. In order to save the girls, he had to make tough choices, and it literally tore him open and left his psyche bloody. Drake had seen the flashbacks he'd had, they were debilitating.

Finn had taken a desk job, knowing he couldn't go out on missions, but every team member of Midnight Delta wanted him back in the field with them.

Drake looked at the file on Mason's desk and he suddenly wanted to be anywhere but there.

"Is that Finn's eval from sniper school?"

"Only Crandall would go from full-blown PTSD, and then enter three months of the most grueling and psychologically stressful training the SEAL teams have to offer. Shit, I tried to talk him out of it. He just gave me that stare of his. I shut my mouth after five sentences."

"Don't leave me in suspense, did he wash out?"

Mason snorted, and flipped open the file. "He was first in his class."

"So why the fuck do you have your panties in a twist? That's awesome." Drake grinned.

Mason scowled, and threw his pen down on the file. "I'll tell you why. Gates, over at the Sniper school is planning on recruiting Finn to be one of the instructors."

Drake whistled. "That's big. That's really big. That's fucking huge."

"Thanks for stating the obvious."

Drake's mind raced. Finn was one of those guys who loved mentoring people, but...

"He's a sneaky bastard. His ability to find a needle in a haystack in the middle of the goddamn jungle or desert has saved our asses on at least six missions that I can count. I mean, we would have been fucked without him. He knows it. Clint tries, but Finn can make things appear out of thin air. He gets a woody doing that stuff. I don't think being an instructor will be as much of a draw."

"It will be if he still has any worries about being detrimental to the team." Mason rubbed the back of his neck, a sure sign he was stressed.

"How the hell can he think he would be a detriment? He just went through the toughest training SEALs have. If he came out first in his class, he has to be at the top of his intellectual and psychological game."

"I get it. You get it. Gates gets it. Hell, the shrink gets it. But if there is one single doubt in Finn's head he'll take the instructor job."

"I would have been more worried about Declan and the Shadow Alliance. You know Dec has been trying to recruit him ever since Finn went on desk duty, don't you?" Drake said.

Mason's eyes went cold. "Yeah, I know it. I called the bastard."

"Finn told you?" Drake was surprised.

"Hell no, he didn't tell me. But I knew Declan would be calling him. I know how that devious fucker's mind works. I told him that Finn was mine and that I'd rip his throat out if he tried to recruit one of my men."

Drake chuckled. He would have loved to have been a fly on the wall for that conversation. "You stopped Declan from taking him, now you want us to double team Finn so he doesn't take Gates up on his offer. Do I have it right?"

"That about sums it up."

"Call him in. If he even thinks about taking the instructor job, I'll beat the shit out of him."

"You might have thirty pounds on him, but he fights dirty. I'd say it'd be even."

"Fine." Drake agreed with Mason's assessment. "I don't have much time though."

Mason raised his eyebrow in question.

"I've got to get back home. I'm waiting on a call back from a realtor." Plus, he was already antsy to get back to Andrew and Karen.

"You're not letting the grass grow under your feet." Mason smiled.

"Clint found it before it went on the market. If I can get in there before a bidding war starts it should be mine. I want to get them to sign papers today."

"That's kind of impulsive isn't it?"

"No, it's in Clint and Lydia's complex. Basically, has the same floorplan only with four bedrooms. Karen loves their place, so it should be a no brainer."

"Well, good luck."

"Call Finn in. Let's get this over with." Drake cracked his knuckles.

Mason pulled out his cell and texted Finn. They waited ten minutes, shooting the shit about Black Dawn's last mission. Finn knocked on the door. He came in sweaty from working out.

"Drake." He grinned enthusiastically. "What pulled you away from Karen and Andrew Mason?"

Drake loved the way his team always used Andrew's middle name. They got a kick out of him naming his son after their lieutenant.

"Something important," Mason said. "I'd ask you to have a seat..."

"I'd decline. I wouldn't want to be the next guy sitting in the chair," Finn agreed.

"So why the hell didn't you tell me that you came in first at sniper school?" Mason asked casually. Drake watched as a flush rose on Finn's Scandinavian features.

"It didn't seem important."

"It sure did to Captain Gates," Mason said with a casual smile. "He hand-delivered your file this morning."

Finn's demeanor changed, became cautious. "He did?"

"Yep. Wanna know why?"

"Yeah." Finn glanced between Mason and Drake, knowing something was up.

"You made a hell of an impression on him. He wants to recruit you."

Finn didn't say anything. Drake watched him carefully. This was classic Finn Crandall. He was going silent, forcing others to spill their guts. But Mason was Mason, and he out silenced him.

"Do you want me to take it?" Finn finally asked.

"God, you're a dumbshit," Drake ground out. "How could you even ask that question?"

"I'm talking to Mase." Finn stared at their commander.

"Finn, this isn't about what I want, this is about what you want," Mason said quietly.

"God, are you a dumbshit, Mason?" Drake roared. "You just got done telling me that you'd do anything to keep Finn on our team. Jesus Christ, you both sound like junior high school girls wanting to know if a boy likes her or not. Fine,

I'll be the middle man. You like each other! Finn, Mason wants you on the team. We all fucking want you on the team. And Mason, Finn wants to be on the team. Do I need to knock your heads together? Because I will."

"This has to be Finn's decision," Mason said stubbornly.

"You are such a girl."

"Do you believe I can hack it?" Finn asked. "I need you to be honest."

"You're a girl too," Drake said with disgust.

"Shut it," Mason clipped out, he turned to Finn. "And you. Do you honestly think I would do *anything* that would endanger my team? Ever? For that matter, do you think I would do anything that would put you in harm's way? I thought you were good before you did sniper school. Now I'm thinking of making you second-in-command, since Drake keeps calling us girls."

For the first time since entering the office there was a hint of a smile on Finn's face.

"I want in on the action. I appreciate Gate's offer but that isn't what I want to do. Maybe when I'm too old for the field." Finn let his voice trail off.

"It's settled then. You're dating." Drake got up and clapped Finn on the back and winked at Mason. "I'm out of here."

Drake left the office, shaking hands with some of the guys on other teams that he hadn't seen since Andrew had been born. His phone rang when he got to his truck. It was Roberta.

"Drake, can you be over there in two hours for a viewing?" she asked.

He looked at his watch. It was going to be tight, but he said yes.

"Are you putting together the offer papers?" he asked.

"Already done." She chuckled.

"You're the best."

"Bring Andrew."

"Huh?" What was she talking about? Drake wondered as he started his truck.

"They'll sign on the dotted line when they see a young family looking to buy their home. Trust me. There'll be no negotiations, they'll just sign. Bring Andrew."

"Okay. You're the boss."

———

"Honey, I'm home," Drake called out as he twirled his keys. He smelled something good coming from the kitchen. God, Wilma could cook, now he understood where Karen had gotten her mad skills with spices.

"Shhhh, Karen's still sleeping," Wilma said coming out of the kitchen.

"Dammit."

"What's wrong, Drake?"

"We need to leave. In a little over an hour we need to be at a townhome to look it over and sign papers to buy it."

Wilma stared at him in shock. "You're not serious."

"As a heart attack."

"I don't know whether to be happy for you, or to say you're crazy."

"Be happy for us. We've been trying to get into this complex since Karen sold her house in Tennessee. She's going to be thrilled."

"Well I'll go put the food away and have it ready to warm up for later. This will give me some alone time with Andrew."

"Actually, Wilma, I was hoping you could go with us.

Our realtor said that having Andrew along would help the sellers sell to us before they put the house on the market. We're kind of using him as baby bait."

"That's terrible."

"Not if it gets him a room of his own. Thanks for cooking dinner," Drake said as he headed down the hall. When he got to the master bedroom he saw that Karen was awake and had Andrew cuddled next to her on the bed.

"You're loud," she said.

"You heard?"

"We have a chance at a townhome?"

"If we can make it over there in time. You up for a day out?"

"Try and stop me. However, I don't like the term baby bait."

Drake reddened. He had regretted it the moment it had come out of his mouth.

"Roger that."

"You did good Drake." Karen was vaguely aware of her mother saying from the backseat of the crew cab truck.

"It was Karen's idea to buy into that complex."

Yay me, Karen thought drowsily as the freeway blew by.

"Then you both did a good job. Piper and Andrew will have their own rooms, and you and Karen can share an office if you want."

Karen smiled as Drake let out a laugh. "She and I are going to be fighting as to whether that is an office or a weight room. She, of course, wants weights."

Karen snorted, then fell asleep. The next thing she knew her door was being opened.

"You carry Andrew, and I'll carry this bundle." She heard Drake say.

"Can walk," Karen said batting away Drake's hands as he unbuckled her seatbelt. He kissed her, and all thought of protesting faded away. His kiss was soft, sweet, and hot. Before she knew it, she was awake. *All* of her was awake.

"There she is," he whispered.

He lifted her out of the truck and pushed closed the door with his shoulder.

"I *can* walk," she breathed into his ear.

"I've liked carrying you from the very first. Remember?" She did. It had been snowing that day in Tennessee. She'd been mesmerized by Piper's big brother from the very first. She settled into his arms and luxuriated in Drake's strength and protection. Soon she was in their room, the heat was on, Drake was helping her out of her clothes.

"Honey, I can undress myself," she gave a sleepy protest. "I'm not an invalid."

"This isn't about you being an invalid. This is about me taking care of you. I used to do this even before you were pregnant. It was like I got to unwrap my own secret present."

Karen melted at his words. She was so lucky. But darn it, she was so tired too.

"Andrew needs to be fed," she said sleepily.

"Your mom's taking him for the night. She's using the stored breast milk."

"S'okay." She smiled as his lips touched hers. So tender. So Drake.

THE TROPICAL BREEZE *drifted through the gauzy curtains, soothing and arousing her body as she looked at the man she* loved. She could hear the ocean from their hotel room. Karen traced the line of Drake's broad shoulders with her eyes, all of those muscles that carried her with ease, that drove her crazy with need.

Her hands clenched into fists, then released and she slowly stroked her hands over the sleek skin of his back.

"Baby, you're playing with fire." His voice sounded like Tennessee whiskey poured over gravel and it feathered another layer of fantasy onto her already heightened senses. Karen continued rubbing her palms up and down Drake's warm flesh. She loved watching how he moved into her touch. She placed a kiss on the middle of his back. How could she resist? She breathed him in.

"Now you've done it." He rolled over in bed and midnight eyes captured hers, they were so hot she thought she would melt. She smiled and raked her nails through the hair on his chest, loving how he shuddered. Drake took her left hand and brought it to his mouth and kissed her palm, she felt it all the way to her knees.

"Drake, I need."

"I know what you need, Sweetheart." He brought took her hands and put them to her sides, and teased the straps of her nightie down her arms. The gown balked in its descent over her full breasts. Drake's eyes glittered as he stared. "God, you're gorgeous." He made her feel beautiful. How did he do that, when she was so much fuller than she had been? The man was amazing.

He pushed the material over the tips of her breasts, and the rasp caused her to gasp. She was so sensitive now. His fingers skimmed over the delicate tracery of veins, so good, so damn good. Then he licked from her areola on up, raining kisses along her collarbone until he bit her earlobe and she muffled a cry.

Karen struggled to get her arms loose of her gown, and when she did, she threaded her fingers through his hair and tugged so *that she got exactly what she needed, his mouth on hers. How could every kiss get better? Hot, wet, and lush, Karen's head spun as she spiraled into need. She pressed herself so close that she hurt.*

"Slow down, Love. We have time."

"No. Now," Karen panted.

He brushed a kiss against her temple, then whispered in her ear. "Let me savor you." He guided her back against the pillows and the velvet breeze brushed against her skin making her ache even more.

Heat and honey flowed through her veins as his calloused fingertips caressed her hips, and held her in place at the same time. "Can you be still?"

She nodded in the dark.

"Karen?"

"Yes," she sighed.

Those talented fingers slid down to her outer thighs. Drake's warm breath awakened every nerve from the tips of her toes to the end of each strand of hair. The pleasure was too much, and she moved again, it wasn't on purpose, but he kept her safe, his hands gently clamping down, keeping her torso in place.

"I need," she said the softest of whispers.

"I know what you need," he whispered back. "I don't want you to hurt. Feeling needy is okay," he said softly, "hurting isn't."

Drake's fingers trailed to the inside of her thighs. So close, but not close enough. "Please," she moaned.

He blew on her over heated flesh, then finally he put his mouth to her, and the rush of heat crowded out all reasonable thought. Karen slammed her feet against the bed and she arched up high then cried out as a wave of both pain and searing pleasure swept through her.

4

"KAREN?" DRAKE WAS AWAKE IN A NANOSECOND WHEN HE heard her cry of pain. He leaned over her trembling body. He could see the tears in her wide emerald eyes. "Honey, where does it hurt? Do we need to get you to the hospital?" She frantically shook her head.

"Karen, talk to me, what's wrong?" She was clearly hurting.

"It was a dream." Her voice was forlorn.

How could a dream give her pain? Then he thought. "Honey, did you move wrong?" He pushed back the covers, and turned on the lamp on the nightstand. "Let me check your incision."

"No." She pushed at his hands. "Please Drake, don't touch me. It's too much."

He held up his hands in surrender. "Baby, I'm not touching you, I promise." What the hell was going on? He watched as tears leaked down her temples. Fucking-A. He needed to check her out, she had to be hurt bad.

"Karen, I need to take a look. You could be bleeding."

"I'm not," she assured him.

"Why are you crying. You're hurting, aren't you?" He watched as she bit her bottom lip, finally she nodded. "Can I look?" She shut her eyes, then nodded. Drake carefully lifted her gown. She wasn't bleeding, which was a huge damned relief. It still made him wince to see where they had cut her open. The incision had gone from red to pink, and right now it was looking a little more swollen than when he'd helped her get ready for bed.

"Karen, I think you put stress on your tummy somehow while you were sleeping."

She turned her head away from him, or was it the light? Drake wasn't sure. She was acting totally out of sorts, and he couldn't figure why. He hated that. He looked down at her stomach again, at the spot where she had been cut open so that Andrew could be given life. He placed a reverent kiss against her healing scar, her body bucked.

"No."

"Honey, tell me what's wrong, I'm begging you."

"I had a dream."

He had to strain to hear her. When he looked up he could see red suffusing her face. Drake gave her a questioning glance, as she pushed down her nightie.

"I dreamed of us. We were...were..." she stuttered.

Many of the puzzle pieces fell into place, including the cry he had heard. "Ah, Honey." He gathered her into his arms, and pulled the covers around them. She burrowed her face against his neck.

"Hold me?"

"I am."

"Hold me tighter," she asked in a soft voice.

He gathered her a little closer, he knew that her breasts and tummy were both sensitive and he'd be damned if he was going to cause her even the slightest bit of discomfort. "Karen, why are you in pain?"

"I arched up."

Yep, that would explain it. He kissed her forehead, and extricated himself from her arms and got out of the bed. "I'm going to get you something for the pain, it'll help you sleep."

"That's probably for the best," she agreed.

He went to the kitchen and came back with a glass of water, then got a pill from her bottle and handed it to her. She took a sip. "Drink it all," he admonished. She sighed, then drank the entire glass. He grinned, then put the glass down. He got back into bed and immediately pulled her back into his arms.

"I love it when you hold me," she said as he reached over her and turned off the light.

"That works out pretty good, because holding you is right up there with lasagna."

She hit his shoulder. Hard. But he got her to laugh, which is what he'd wanted.

"What's the ETA on sexy time? I'm not talking sexy '*sexy*' time. I figure that's months away. But me pleasuring my woman sexy time?" Drake asked.

Karen's hand started a path down his torso, but he stopped her. "Honey, we're not going there. If I can't reciprocate, then my cock is on lock-down."

He saw her green eyes widen in the darkness. "Now that's just plain stupid," she protested.

"Karen, since meeting you, being with you, loving you, how could I want anything else but the magic of us being together? I'm not talking the sex act, I'm talking us loving one another. When your body's ready for more, then I'll be ready for something more."

Again, she shoved her face into his neck and he felt her hot breath saw in and out against his skin. "I love you," she whispered softly.

"Love you more. Let's get some sleep before your mom hands off the little guy." Karen's breathing changed to rhythmic sighs. Having her warm and lush body nestled close to his had a predictable effect on him, but he was just going to have to be content with having his woman and child near and safe, after all, that was what truly made him happy. And on that note Drake followed Karen into sleep.

———

DRAKE GOT up before dawn and went for a run. When he was back he slid into the bathroom without waking Karen. He wanted to beat Wilma to the kitchen. She had been making breakfast since she got there. He wanted a chance to spoil both Eastman women. What's more, he wanted to see if he could find out what was bothering her before Karen woke. Wilma had been upset before they had left for the townhome yesterday.

He got out the waffle iron and turned it on, then he started to core and cut up the strawberries. He wasn't surprised when Wilma wandered in when the coffee started to brew, and the bacon started to fry. She was an early riser.

"Good morning," she said brightly.

"Andrew's still conked out?"

"I took him into Karen while you were out. They both fell back asleep after she fed him, but if I know my girl, the smell of bacon will get her out of bed."

"Hopefully we'll have a chance to talk before she gets up."

Wilma tilted her head in question.

"I think something's bothering you, and I want to know if there was anything I could do to help. Is it about James?"

Wilma's shoulders sagged. Damn, Drake hadn't wanted to be right. "Is it his health?"

"We're not sure. The doctor called and said some of his numbers were elevated and they wanted him to come back in for a full workup. Jim is going with him today."

It was obvious that Wilma wished she was going with her husband. No wonder she was conflicted. James had suffered from an aggressive bone cancer four years ago and lost part of his leg. "Do you need to get home? I'm perfectly capable of taking care of Karen if you need to leave."

"She's still weak, even if she won't admit it, and you have a job to go back to."

"I'm on family leave."

"Karen told me that you haven't left her in five months, how much longer can you afford to take off?"

Captain Hale, Mason's commander, had been very accommodating, but his team needed him. It killed him, hearing about the last three missions that he hadn't been a part of. "The clock started again when Andrew was born."

"That's not what I'm talking about. How much longer can you handle staying at home?"

Damn, she was good. He said as much.

"Honey, I've raised three boys."

"With you here I've been able to get to the base and get in some training. But what you haven't taken into account is how much I adore my wife and child. Spending time with them means the world to me."

Wilma's laugh warmed the kitchen. She walked over and wrapped her arms around Drake. "I love it when you refer to Karen as your wife."

"Well, she is. Regardless of the ceremony, she is my wife

in all ways. Shit, we should have gotten married sooner." Goddamn bedrest. "But you're deflecting. Do you need to get back to Alaska?"

"We'll see what today's tests say."

"Let me phrase this another way. Do you *want* to get back to Alaska?" Wilma stepped back and sighed.

"Yes. But I adore Karen and Andrew too. Leaving them isn't easy."

"But you want to go."

Wilma nodded.

"Then you need to go. Why don't you check on flights while I finish making breakfast?"

"I'll do it after. You need to turn that bacon." Drake looked over his shoulder. Shit, she was right.

"Piper should be home from class in a couple of hours, I'll be fine until then."

Drake crossed his arms and stared at her. Andrew took that moment to let out a cry from his infant seat.

"I've got him," they both said at the same time.

"Drake, Honey, you know you want to go to the base. This is a drill you designed, you know you want to be there to run it with your team."

"No, I don't." She watched him lie. "Mason will tell me the results." He extracted Andrew from the small chair, and even though she was frustrated with her man, her heart melted a little seeing him hold their son.

"Drake, I've seen the doctor, she told me I was progressing nicely."

"It's only been three weeks."

God, she hated it when he jutted out his chin like that.

She just knew that Andrew was going to do the same thing whenever he got in a stubborn mood.

He came over and put his arm around her, so the three of them were in their own little world. "Karen, I'm still having trouble with the fact that I almost lost you. You might think that three weeks has been a long time, but for me it was just a moment ago, and I break into a cold sweat whenever I think about it. I'm sure I'll get over it, but can you bear with me a little longer?"

"Drake, you love your job, this isn't a career, this is a calling. I'm perfectly fine." Still no response. She rose up on tiptoe and kissed his chin. Looking up into his eyes, she said, "I love you."

"I love you more."

"We need to come up with a compromise."

His eyes turned thoughtful. Then he released her and took out his phone.

"Drake, I don't need a babysitter," she said sharply.

"This is the compromise. You were fine when it was your mother," he reminded her.

"That's because it was my *mother*, mothering me. I'm used to that."

"Are you still upset about her keeping things from you? Everything turned out fine with your dad's test results."

"I'm upset that *both* of you kept things from me. I'm a grown woman."

"You figured it out in five minutes."

"Of course, I did. Mom wouldn't have left for any other reason. Geez, you two need to work on better cover stories."

"This time I'm not even trying to come up with one. I'm being up front about you needing someone to stay with you. Don't I get points?" he wheedled.

Karen sighed. He was in his stubborn mode and he was

charming, she was doomed. She knew when to give in. Drake spoke into his phone, "Call Sophia Gault." He put Sophia on speaker.

"Hi Drake," she answered.

"Hey Sophia. I was wondering if you would mind coming over and keeping Karen company for a bit, while I go to the base today. Piper's still at school."

"I would love to. I'm here at the food bank with the girls. We're just finishing packing the weekend rucksacks for the kids. Did you know it's over six hundred here in San Clemente?" Drake winced. His family often had to rely on a food pantry back in Tennessee when he was growing up, he knew the hardship those six hundred children were going through.

"Hey Drake! We'll all come over," Karen heard another woman call out. It took a moment for her to recognize Angie Donatelli's voice. She was Finn Crandall's fiancée. Now it was Karen's turn to wince. The idea of hosting a bunch of women held no appeal.

"Tell Karen we'll stop by the café and bring food. She doesn't need to worry about a thing," Sophia assured them.

"I'm listening Sophia," Karen said. "It's okay, I have plenty of things to eat."

"I insist. You just relax. We'll be there in less than an hour. I can't wait to get my hands on Andrew Mason." She and Drake smiled at one another. It was true, Sophia hadn't really had a chance to hold Mason's namesake since the hospital.

"I'll see you soon," Karen said resignedly.

"Wait, what should I bring for you to eat? I'm ordering from the diner."

"Anything but salad." Karen answered. Now she was

perking up. Comfort food from the diner sounded damn good.

"Chicken and dumplings? Meatloaf?" Sophia asked.

"Yes," Drake answered for Karen. "She'll have both. She hasn't been eating enough."

"Oh for goodness sake. I have been eating more than enough," Karen said with exasperation.

Drake leaned in and whispered in her ear. "You're breastfeeding. The doc said you have to consume a ton of calories and you're not."

She opened her mouth to argue, then she shut it. He was right. She'd been too tired to eat. That was so not good. "Sophia, bring a milkshake too, would you?" Karen requested.

"What flavor?"

"The only kind there is," Karen said.

"Gotcha." Sophia laughed. "Chocolate it is."

Drake kissed the side of her neck, said goodbye to Sophia, and hung up the phone.

"I need to get changed," Karen whispered.

"Too bad you don't need help anymore. I miss that."

She started to laugh, and then he cupped her face. "Karen, I'm not joking."

"Oh," she breathed. His sexuality had often taken her by surprise, and this was one of those times.

"Yeah, oh." He caught her bottom lip with his teeth and caressed it with his tongue. She trembled and her core melted.

Andrew let out a small cry. Nothing major, just a, 'I'm here, quit ignoring me,' cry.

"I think I caught a whiff of something. It smells like your son needs some attention." Karen's voice was weak.

Drake sniffed and laughed.

"Little man, you're powerful. And your timing sucks." Drake picked him up. "Let's get you cleaned up. You're about to have a bunch of admirers to entertain." Andrew's head bobbed against his father's massive chest. It was almost as if he were nodding in agreement. Give him just a little bit of time, and he'd be just as big a flirt as Drake, Karen thought with a smile.

By the time the doorbell rang, she and Andrew were ready for guests and Drake was ready to leave. He opened the door.

"Hey big guy," Lydia Hildalgo said with a huge smile. Her hands were full, and Drake grabbed the take-out bags, and put them on the bar between the living room and kitchen. Lydia's sister Beth Preston came in behind her along with Angie Donatelli. Rylie Jones and Sophia were laughing about something as they brought up the rear.

Karen was impressed how Andrew calmly took in the commotion. He didn't fuss in her arms, instead his head moved constantly, almost as if he wanted to see what was going on. Three weeks old and he was just like his father.

"I expected Evie to be here," Drake said.

"Aiden's team just got off a six-day maneuver. He's home today. I have no earthly idea what your sister could possibly be doing," Lydia said tongue-in-cheek.

"Shut up, my sister is a virgin." Drake glowered.

"A married virgin." Karen grinned.

"Exactly." He pulled Andrew from Karen's hold, and cuddled him close, then kissed his forehead. "You be good for your Mama. No back talk, ya hear?" Karen loved it when his Southern came out. Still holding their son, he touched his lips to hers. Heat flared, no matter that they had an audience, she curled her arms around his neck.

When they broke apart, he gave her his trademark slow

grin. "I love you, Lady. You be good and don't do too much, ya hear?"

"Drake, one day the doctor will give me the green light to have sex, but at the rate you're going, you won't get any."

Lydia and Rylie burst out laughing.

"Okay, okay, I'll back off. Did anyone ever tell you you're beautiful when you're angry?"

"Oh my God, you must really like being celibate."

He leaned in and kissed her. Really kissed her. The man could kiss. He lifted his head and gazed down at her and grinned. "That knife cuts both ways."

She laughed. She couldn't help it. He was outrageous.

"I'll be back tonight." He turned to the ladies who had been watching with avid interest. "Take care of my woman."

"God, he's a caveman." Lydia shook her head sadly.

"What are you talking about, yours is too." Her sister, Beth, nudged her in the ribs with her elbow.

"We'll take good care of her," Sophia promised. "Now let me hold Andrew Mason." She held out her arms. Drake carefully transferred Andrew into Sophia's waiting arms. Her smile turned golden. Most of the other women gathered round. He turned back to Karen and mouthed *I love you.* Then he walked out the door.

Rylie grabbed bags from the cooing women and headed toward the kitchen. Karen followed her.

Karen took the time in the kitchen to ask Rylie how her foster siblings were doing. It was a complicated story, but she and Dare had custody of three children ranging in ages seventeen to eight.

"The two oldest like San Diego a lot better than Oklahoma. Georgie desperately misses the woman who used to take care of him when I was out of town. We SKYPE almost every day with Mrs. Whitehawk, but it doesn't matter. I think it's the autism, because he can't touch and feel her, he can't comprehend that it's her on the screen."

Karen hadn't met Georgie, but she'd heard about him from Dare. Both he and Rylie were devoted to the eight-year-old.

"Has he started school?"

Rylie brightened. "Dare found a place for him, and he attends three times a week, he's acclimating really well. I never thought that would be possible."

"That's wonderful," Karen said.

"Are you going back to teaching?" Rylie asked.

"I'm going to wait for Andrew to get just a little older, then I'm going to get certified in California. After that, yes, I'm going back to teaching. I love it."

"I could see you in front of a class." Rylie smiled.

"Quit yakking in there, the party's out here," Lydia called from the living room.

Karen took a sip of her milkshake as she headed toward the living room and realized she was starving. Lydia saw it and laughed.

"Rylie, we need to feed the Mama. Where are the dumplings?"

Soon everything was plated, and everybody was eating their food and talking in the living room.

The conversation soon turned to Karen's wedding. Sophia told Karen some of the ideas she had for the desserts and Karen told the girls some of the problems she was having with the caterer. Eventually they started talking about the men in their lives.

"You do realize, you're marrying the biggest caveman of them all, don't you?" Lydia asked.

"I might have the biggest caveman of them all, but it's my

job to make sure he has a safe place to land. I make sure I'm always watching his back too. It's a partnership, Ladies."

"I like to think that I coddle Clint," Lydia said.

"You would." Sophia laughed.

Sophia's phone rang. Then Lydia's. They both went for their purses.

Karen listened as they both started taking calls from their men. Then Rylie's phone rang, and she handed Andrew to Karen. When Angie and Beth's phone rang, Karen knew what was going on. The men had been called on a mission. She cuddled Andrew close and waited for her phone to ring.

All the women walked around the apartment to different spots for privacy, one to the kitchen, one down the hall, one to the balcony and Lydia turned her back on the couch and whispered into her phone. Karen got up and walked past Rylie to her bedroom and shut the door. She put Andrew down in the bassinette and called Drake.

"Hey, Honey," he answered. "Is everything okay?"

"I was going to ask you the same thing."

"Sure, why wouldn't it be?"

"Because, once again you're not going on a mission."

He didn't answer.

"Drake?"

"What do you want me to say?"

"I want you to say that you're going with your team members," Karen said in frustration. "I want you to say that you're going to do the job you love."

"I am going to do what I love, which is stay home with my woman and son." She heard just as much frustration in his voice as there had been in hers.

"Dammit, Drake. I had my doctor's visit. Everything is fine." She paced around the bed, trying but failing to keep her voice down. "Piper's here with me during the evenings and weekends. This is your job."

"I have family leave. I'm taking it."

God the man was so block-headed she needed a hammer and chisel to get through.

"I refuse to be an anchor."

"How could you and our son *ever* be an anchor?" His voice was rising too.

"You've told me how your team acts as a unit. How every one of you is an integral part of a mission. Well I know you. I *know* you. They need you, Drake Avery. Get your ass on that plane or boat, or whatever, and go with them."

Andrew started crying at her raised voice. She went over and patted his tummy, it didn't help.

"Ship. They're called ships. And we'd be going on a plane. What's wrong with Andrew?"

Then she heard it. This wasn't about her needing him to stay home to take care of her, he was having trouble leaving because of her near-death experience and he was loathe to leave their son. God, how stupid was she?

"He doesn't like it when his mommy is arguing with his daddy."

"We're not arguing," Drake protested.

"Yes, we are.," Karen sighed. "Get on the ship."

"I'm going on a plane."

She let out a deep breath. The knot in her chest unravelling. "So, you're going?"

She heard his sigh through the telephone. "Didn't you just give me an order? I live to serve."

She giggled. "I'll remember that when I'm finally healed up."

"Oh, so I'm not on the naughty list anymore. You're going to give me the go ahead?" he teased.

"You know I can't resist you," she teased back.

Magically, Andrew settled at her laugh. She sat on the side of the bed and cuddled the phone close, waiting for Drake to continue to talk.

"You're sure you're going to be alright?"

She rolled her eyes. "I'm absolutely positive."

"I worry about you."

"Drake, who *don't* you worry about?"

"Clint. I don't worry about Clint."

She laughed. "You have your 'go bag'?" she asked, referring to the bag that contained everything he needed to leave at the drop of a hat. He normally kept it in his truck, but he might have taken it out since Andrew was born.

"Yeah, Baby, I have it."

"Do you need to leave immediately?"

"I do," he said quietly.

"We love you."

"I love you more," his Southern accent was thick.

"Stay safe."

"Always."

5

"IT WAS A COORDINATED EFFORT," CAPTAIN HALE SAID grimly. He was briefing Midnight Delta and Black Dawn. The pictures on the screen showed the explosion at the airport in Douala, Cameroon.

"How many casualties?" Mason asked.

"Over one hundred, at least twenty dead. The car bomb at the Nigerian Embassy killed three of our marines. They stopped it before it made it to the building itself."

"Hooyah," the SEALs shouted.

"My sentiments exactly. Boko Haram has taken credit for both incidents. One thing that both Nigeria and Cameroon are working to keep under wraps is the fact that a girl's orphanage on the Cameroon side of the border was overrun."

"Fuck." Drake's heart sank. The high-profile kidnapping of over two hundred girls from a school in 2014 was just one incident, there were many more that flew under the radar.

"How many girls?" Finn asked. Mason's head turned swiftly to stare at Finn, he knew how badly affected he had been when young girls had been trafficked in the past.

"It's not known," Captain Hale said.

"What's our mission?" Mason asked. Drake could read the waves coming off his entire team, they all wanted to go after the girls.

"The CIA has intel that there is going to be a shipment of arms coming into either Ekong, Nigeria or Mundemba, Cameroon. I need both locations covered."

Well that explained why both teams were being briefed. Come on Cameroon. He had a feeling that was where the tangos were going to be. He wanted them. He wanted them badly. He felt heat on his neck. He turned and saw Clint staring at him. He mouthed *Cameroon*. Yep, it was a lock.

Gray Tyler, the lieutenant of Black Dawn spoke up. "Is our mission contained to just stopping the shipment?"

Captain Hale looked at Gray, then at Mason. "Your mission is to stop the shipment first and foremost. As always, I trust my teams to get the job done. I understand that every mission is fluid, and you will do what is right."

Damn, Captain Hale had tacitly given them permission to save the girls if at all possible, as long as they stopped the shipment. Mason caught his eye. He could read his mind. He'd planned to help the girls no matter what. *Righteous.*

"You're flying out in an hour. Black Dawn will be going to the airstrip the CIA identified in Nigeria. Mason, you and your team will be headed to Cameroon. You'll be sharing transport to the Margaret Ekpo Airport in Nigeria. There'll be choppers waiting to take you close to your destinations."

"Was the orphanage close to the Margaret Ekpo Airport?" Aiden asked.

"The orphanage was in Amoto, Cameroon, which is almost exactly sixty clicks from Mundemba, but it would take you ten hours to get there from the airport because the

Cross River National Park is basically a jungle. That's why you need the choppers."

"I'm leaving the rest of the coordination up to the two of you. I'll need reports as often as possible when you hit the ground. Do you have any questions?"

"Who's our intelligence liaison?" Mason asked.

"You've got two. Sheila Baker is CIA, she's going with you, she'll be here soon. Then there is Edwin Marsh, he's with the Nigerian Embassy, he'll be meeting you at the airport. By the time you get there, he'll have something set up."

Gray asked what Drake was thinking. "Are they setting up a command center near the airport?"

"That's the plan."

Thank all that was holy. Drake remembered one clusterfuck of a mission where a CIA operative thought he could keep up with the SEALs. He'd almost gotten Jack killed.

Captain Hale left the briefing room and Gray huddled up with Mason. Aiden gave a head jerk to Drake, and he followed him to the back of the room.

"Yeah?" Drake asked.

"The girls?" Aiden asked. "They're not going to have gotten far."

"Depends what CIA has to tell us about the rendezvous point for the arms deal. Hell, if they take them into the jungle it's anybody's game," Drake pointed out.

Aiden nodded.

"But we agree on one thing. It's not going to be like that school three years ago. They're not going to disappear."

"Amen, brother," Aiden said.

"Don't call me that. It gives me the heebie jeebies." Drake shuddered.

Aiden grinned. He liked rubbing in the fact that he'd married Drake's sister as often as possible. "I wonder how Karen's brothers are going to take to having you in the family."

"They're going to love me," Drake said positively.

"Sure, they are," Aiden taunted.

SHEILA MADE it just in time to board the plane. She was still getting information from Langley at the beginning of the sixteen-hour flight, and they decided she'd brief them when they were closer to Africa. They strapped into the plane for the long flight. Drake sat between Finn and Jack. Mason was on the other side of Finn, they did it on purpose, they were taking his temperature. This couldn't get any worse. The thing that had sent Finn into a tailspin in the first place had been young girls in the slave trade in Canada, so the fact that they were going on a mission where young girls had been kidnapped by Boko Haram had to be his worst nightmare.

Mason played it cool. He leaned back and closed his eyes. Drake waited until everybody was asleep, except for Mason. He knew he was faking it. Then Drake waded in, because he couldn't help himself. The blunt approach was always his methodology. He stared at Finn until he finally rolled his head against the headrest to look at him.

"Drop it, Avery."

"Are you going to wig out?"

"Jesus. You have the tact of an elephant in a dollhouse."

"That's a bull in a china shop," Drake shot back.

"I said what I meant. You're worse than a bull. Are you

going to tell me you're not torn apart about those girls in the hands of those animals?"

Drake didn't answer. How could he? He had six younger sisters and a four-year-old niece. It made him sick, but they had a mission to complete. Stopping those weapons meant that they would be saving the next school or orphanage, and the next, and so on.

"Yes, it makes me want to puke, but I'm going to be able do the job. Are you?"

Finn shook his head, then he grinned. "I've missed you and our special little times together."

What?

"No matter how bad it got, you never treated me with kid gloves. Even Mase watched his words, you never have."

"Just answer the fucking question."

"If I didn't know. And I mean *know* that I was rock solid, I wouldn't be on this plane. We're going to stop the shipment, then we are going to rescue those girls and annihilate those fuckers." Finn's smile was fierce.

"Hooyah," Drake said.

"Now that you're done being my shrink am I allowed to get some sleep?"

"Yep." Drake shut his eyes, and leaned back against the hard headrest. Images of Andrew and Karen filled his head as he willed himself to sleep.

DRAKE HADN'T SEEN Mason so pissed in years. His face was carved out of stone. Sheila had given the two lieutenants and their seconds the lowdown on the plane. Which meant that Mason, Gray, Drake and Aiden felt confident they knew what they needed to get done on the mission. Then they got to the airport and Edwin Marsh pushed his way into the picture.

Everyone knew many of the embassy members were CIA, and that's who Marsh was. Turns out, he was the head CIA guy in Nigeria. He started countermanding Captain Hale's orders right from the get-go.

"The Boko Haram won't do any kind of pick-up in Cameroon, they will stick to Nigeria. That's their preferred area of operation."

"They are already way out of their preferred area of operation. They're usually in the desert, instead they're here in the jungle. We need to listen to Langley on this."

"I don't care if they're south. They'll still stick to Nigeria."

"What are you talking about? Even when they're in the North, they dip into Cameroon all the damn time. Look Marsh, Langley has a source. That's all I'm at liberty to say. That source says the Haram have two points of entry in the South, those are airfields in Ekong, Nigeria and Mundemba, Cameroon."

"Why wasn't I told about an informant?" Edwin was outraged.

"It was need to know," Sheila responded.

"I don't give a shit what Langley says, there is a group of Boko Haram in Nigeria that just took a shot at the embassy, and then there's the group in Cameroon who took the girls from the orphanage in Amoto. The Haram that has the new stash of girls will be too damn busy to go to an airfield, if you get my meaning." The way he said that made Drake's skin crawl. The idea that the terrorists would be hurting those girls turned his stomach. "Trust me, I know both sect leaders. There's Sani and there's Yemisi. Sani has more power than Yemisi, he's going to be the one dealing with the arms."

"These aren't our orders. We are going to cover both airstrips," Mason said, his voice was stone cold.

"No, you're not. Sani is your target. End of discussion. Yemisi is not a big enough fish, trust me, I know what I'm doing." The man was a pompous ass.

"The airfield in Mundemba has been recently cleared, we have satellite imaging that shows that." Sheila tried explaining.

"You also have imaging that shows the airfield in Ekong has been cleared. You will not go after Yemisi. This conversation is over." Edwin Marsh crossed his arms and stared at everyone in the room.

"Seems to me like your dismissy Yemisi awful quick." Clint rhymed the two words, making a joke. Drake smothered a laugh.

"This is nothing to laugh at," Marsh shouted as he turned, trying to figure out who said what.

"That's enough," Mason's voice cut through the room. "You're right it's not a laughing matter. Marsh, we have our orders, and Ms. Baker's highly reliable intelligence. We are going to be following those. We thank you for your attendance today. You are dismissed."

"Dismissy," Clint said just loudly enough for Drake to hear. Drake almost lost it.

"I outrank Sheila," Marsh sputtered.

"Hunter, show Edwin the door," Lieutenant Gray said to his biggest SEAL.

Drake enjoyed watching Hunter Diaz all but shove the wide-eyed Marsh out of the room.

"Ms. Baker, is there anything you would like to add before we board the choppers?" Mason asked.

"Can I take you back to Langley?" she said pointing to Hunter. "You would come in real handy."

Hunter grinned.

THE BLACK DAWN SEAL team boarded their helicopter and Clint nudged Drake. "You know the action is in Cameroon, right?"

"Yeah, I feel it too," Drake agreed.

"Quit the girl talk and climb aboard," Finn shouted above the roar of the rotors. Drake grinned. Finn Crandall was definitely back.

They climbed aboard for twenty click trip to the Mundemba airstrip. They were going to have to hike in. It'd been awhile since Drake had been out to play in the jungle. The others had a recent mission in Costa Rica, so they had a leg up. Not that he'd ever admit it. Jungle schmungle, he could outdo everyone on this team.

An hour later he was breathing hard, but he was near the head of the pack. Jack was up ahead on point and Drake was beside Mason who was acting like he was out walking his goddamn dog or some shit. Drake put a grin on his face. Mason glanced over at him and smiled. Fucker knew he was faking it. Well, fake it 'til you make it. That was his motto. Despite their fast pace, they were silent. They wanted to get close to the airfield before dawn so they could check things out.

Like a ghost, Jack appeared in front of them, calling a halt. Finn, Clint, and Dare, who had only been a few yards behind Drake, and Mason gathered around Jack.

"We have company," he said in a subvocal whisper. "Five armed men are asleep against the trees on this side of the airstrip. I'm assuming they're the guards."

Mason nodded. "Time to spread out and see what we've got. Do a headset check," he whispered.

After that was done, they parted ways.

Drake took the far north end of the airfield. It had to be the end where the plane would land because there was plenty of room to turn around. He found just one guard. This guy was actually awake. He reported in to the rest of the SEAL team. When Mason had them gather back at the rendezvous point, they had counted sixteen Boko Haram soldiers, and according to Dare there were three beat-to-shit jeeps on the far side of the field.

"The leader was with one of the jeeps. He was speaking in French to two other men with him, but was speaking Arabic over the radio."

"What was he saying?" Mason asked.

"He was apologizing to whoever was on the radio. Apparently, it was his brother who overran the orphanage and leadership is pissed."

"Anything about the weapons shipment?"

"Nothing."

"Clint, you need to get ahold of Dex, and find out what their team found at Ekong."

Clint nodded.

They hunkered down, finding a good spot to hide, and waited for an incoming report from Black Dawn. It took two hours, but finally it came in.

"They have nine guards on their airstrip. They also have a fuel truck. Sounds legit," Clint reported.

"Six of one, half dozen of another," Drake said. There was no way to call which airfield was going to be used to unload the weapons. They would both have to be on alert. According to Sheila, the delivery was going to go down in two days. Drake was itching to search for the missing girls, but Clint had already done the calcs and the Amoto Orphanage was sixty clicks from where they were. What were the chances that the forty-five girls would have travelled this way? Still, he knew they would be keeping an eye out.

"I HATE THE RAIN. I hate the rain. I hate the fucking rain."

Drake looked at Clint, and watched as water dripped off the end of his nose. If anybody else bitched as much about the rain, he would have throat punched him, but Clint Archer had every right to complain. Drake vividly remembered the grueling five days he'd carried Lydia Hildalgo through the rainy jungle in Mexico. He wouldn't accept anyone else's help, step after step, mile after mile, he carried her like she was a gift from God.

Drake would never admit this to anyone, not even to Karen, but he had been sure that Lydia was going to die. Finn had done everything medically possible to save her, but Drake believed it was Clint's will that had kept her alive.

Yep, no wonder Clint hated the rain.

"It'll let up soon," Drake assured his friend.

Clint peered over at Drake. "I'm out of my mind. I'm so into myself, I didn't even think about you. How are you coping?"

Drake pretended not to understand. "I like the rain. Fuck, this is nothing compared to a Tennessee rainstorm."

"Cut the shit, Avery. I'm talking about being away from your son. Hell, I can't believe I'm even saying that. I would have thought you would have been the last one of us with a kid."

"What do you mean by that? I'm the perfect guy to be a father."

Clint snorted so hard, that water sprayed out of his nose.

"I resent that," Drake said. "I'm the oldest brother of six girls."

"You've been an insensitive jackass most of the time I've known you," Clint countered.

"Doesn't mean I wasn't right ninety-nine percent of the time, that's why I'm second-in-command. Which proves I'm perfect father material."

"I'm wrong, you're not an insensitive jackass, you're a megalomaniac. I feel sorry for young Andrew. Thank God Mason is his namesake, he has a fighting chance."

Drake grinned and so did Clint. Drake was happy his friend was no longer thinking about the rain and Lydia's near-death experience.

"Did I hear y'all talking about you naming Andrew after Mason and not me?" Jack asked.

"How the hell could you hear us?" Clint asked suspiciously.

Drake wondered the same damn thing. What with the rain and the two of them whispering, they shouldn't have been overheard.

"My stepdad always said I could hear a deer fart in the woods when we went out hunting," Jack said.

Drake wasn't laughing. They shouldn't have been heard. He gave Jack a hard look.

Dare duckwalked over in the mud. Even in the dark, Drake could see he was grinning. What the fuck?

"Jack, quit messing with them. Drake's getting pissed. Next thing you know, he'll be throwing a punch." Dare turned to him and Clint. "Hey, Bonehead, your mic was on. For the record, Clint's right, you have an uncanny ability to insert your foot in your mouth at the most inopportune moments."

Drake switched off his microphone, and turned on Dare. "That's bullshit, I just have the balls to say the things to your women that you won't man up and say. I call them on their shit."

"Yeah, you did such a great job that Rylie went off the grid for months before I could find her again," Dare said heatedly.

Drake winced. He still regretted that one.

"None of that matters anymore," Jack said.

"What do you mean?" Clint said. "I have my own story to tell, he wasn't a peach with Lydia either."

Jack chuckled. "He's a fallen man. As a matter of fact, he's fallen further than the rest of us. He has Karen, and that little kindergarten teacher is schooling him."

Every man surrounding Drake broke into a wide grin. He flipped them all off. That made their grins even larger.

"Okay, enough chit chat, time for another check of the airstrip, we need to make sure nothing's changed. Tomorrow morning is when the shipment is supposed to fly in," Drake said to his men. Out of the corner of his eye, he saw Mason give a nod. Damn, if anybody could hear him without his mic on, it would be his lieutenant. The man was spooky.

Finn broke away from Mason and left as well. Then Drake went to go talk to his leader.

"They're going to be coming tomorrow morning," Mason said.

"You sound sure."

"I have a feeling."

It was foolish to discount Mason's feelings. "When the team gets back, we'll huddle up and strategize."

Mase nodded. "You have a plan, don't you?" Drake asked.

"Mostly. Like Captain Hale said, it's going to have to be fluid. They won't land unless they see the Haram waiting for them, so we can't take them out ahead of time."

Drake agreed.

"The rain would definitely be to our advantage," Mason mused.

"Damn right. So are Jack and Finn. Put them in some trees and they could take out almost everybody before they knew what hit them. I'll go check out the North side of the airstrip again and report back."

"Good."

Drake left Mason, then slowly and quietly made his way through the wet jungle. Near the edge of the airstrip the vegetation was cut back. He didn't see his guard sitting against his tree. Maybe he was sick of getting his ass wet and was up and walking around. With his night vision goggles he could see clearly, and found no sign of the guard. He did see the three guards that Clint normally reported on. Drake continued to look.

It was the coppery smell that warned him. Even with the rain and the monkey shit, the smell of blood was distinctive when you were about to step in it. He looked down and saw not one, but two bodies. He recognized his guard. The two men had been eviscerated. Cut open stem to stern. Somebody was making a point.

He made his way back to Mason. He was the last man there.

"Report," Mason said curtly.

"My guy, and another had been killed. Butchered. My guess is that somebody was trying to show the others that this could happen to them if they made him unhappy."

"Finn ran into the same thing."

"So how many are we down to?" Drake asked.

"Eleven."

"Our odds just got better," Drake said.

"Roger that."

"Clint, find out if Black Dawn is running into the same thing." Clint nodded and went over to his backpack. They waited in silence for him to come back.

"Nope, everything is status quo on their end."

"We've got a wildcard here, instead of two on watch, I want three, while the other three sleep, then we'll trade off," Mason ordered.

Everyone nodded.

"Did you scope out the trees you want to shoot from?" he asked Finn and Jack, the two best sharpshooters in the team. Both men nodded. They had coordinated where they would be shooting from for maximum coverage of the airstrip.

"I don't want anyone in close range unless we need to. But God knows what kind of weapons they'll have on the plane that they can deploy, so we'll need to be ready to stop them."

"On it," Drake said.

"Okay, get some rest. I'll take first watch with Clint and Dare," Mason said.

They nodded.

6

Everybody's instincts had been right, the plane was coming into this airfield. It was the smaller Antanov cargo plane. When the plane shuddered to a stop, members of Boko Haram swarmed out of their hiding spots, rifles raised over their heads, and shouting in triumph. Two of the three jeeps were driven onto the make-shift runway. Soon the only thing heard was the sounds of the jungle and the propellers of the plane winding down.

"We've got a problem," Drake heard Dare's voice over the headset. "I'm close enough to the leader's jeep that I can hear him. He's on the radio, and he's expecting a truck. We've got more company coming."

"Stay in positions," Mason said. "Dare continue to report. Jack, you're on that side of the airstrip, let us know if you can see anything from your position in that tree."

"Roger."

Drake watched as the rear cargo door opened revealing two blond men holding AK-47s directed at the terrorists. He wasn't all that surprised until a third man holding an M-16 appeared. In this part of the world, AK-47s were the gun of choice by everyone but Americans.

"Are you seeing this?" Finn asked.

"Yep," Jack drawled. "Seems like we got us a good ole American boy."

More Boko Haram came out of the jungle and up to the plane. One large man was holding an AK-47 as well, and he shot into the sky. It didn't have any effect on the three men standing on the gangway of the plane. He ran up to the plane and screamed at the three white men. The man with the M-16 shot him in the head.

"Dare, report," Mason commanded.

"The leader was watching. He doesn't seem all that upset that his guy bought it. Hold on, he's calling out on the radio. He's arranging a meet for tonight. Some name I can't pronounce. Let's hope it's with the girls." It seemed like forever that Drake stood there behind his tree in the rain watching the standoff. Finally, Dare spoke again. "The truck should be here any minute. The leader's going to go out to the plane."

"About fucking time," Drake muttered. Slowly the jeep made its way over the muddy ground, and then the leader deliberately rolled the wheels of the vehicle over the dead man and came to a halt in front of the open cargo bay. He called out, his English had a definite French accent.

"Who is Armstrong?"

"Who's asking?" One of the two blond men with the AK-47s shouted.

"I am Samuel Yemisi. I lead the Boko Haram."

The man with the M-16 shouted with laughter. Not a good move. Mounted to the top of the jeep was a machine gun. There was a big guy, who looked pretty fucking grumpy, manning the gun. "Don't give me that shit," the same man continued. "You're nothing but a sect leader."

"You're surrounded. I won't hesitate to have you killed," Yemisi yelled. "Then I will take the weapons and I won't have to pay you."

"This plane is rigged to blow. This isn't our first rodeo," the American said with a shrug. "That's our insurance policy."

"Insurance policy?"

"This plane is set with explosives, I press the trigger on my belt, the plane blows. It takes out everything in a quarter mile radius. So you better pay or we all die."

"You wouldn't dare," Yemisi said.

"Try me."

"I don't think he's kidding, it's what I would do," Finn said.

"He's not kidding," Mason said grimly. "It's a Decault Group tactic. Neither you or Drake were with us on that mission. If Clint hadn't acted so quickly a couple of months ago, we wouldn't be here to tell the story."

"Was this Costa Rica?" Drake asked.

"Yep," Clint said. "You guys have been missing out on all the fun shit."

"Jack or Finn, do you think you could take him out before he hits the trigger?"

"Nope, not from this angle." Jack said.

"If he would come forward another step, I've got him," Finn assured the team.

"So that stops the weapons deal, but how do we find the girls?" Dare asked.

There was silence on the radio. That was one of the things Drake appreciated the most about his team. It wasn't that they were waiting for Mason to come up with the answer, they were waiting for *anyone* to come up with a plan.

"It was Yemisi's brother who had them?" Clint said.

"Yep," Dare confirmed.

"Then we have to let him get away." Drake could hear the excitement in Clint's voice. He was on a roll.

"On foot," Drake quickly said. "I'm sure as hell not going to try to keep up with a jeep."

"Remember, our real job is to stop this weapons exchange," Mason reminded them.

"It'll be nice to take out another one of Decault's operations," Dare put in. "They're a scourge."

"Kills me that they have an American with them," Jack said.

"According to some sources, this is an American operation, not European," Mason told them.

Drake knew they were all killing time, watching the stand-off out on the airfield. There wasn't a goddamn thing they could do but see what would happen. Yemisi wanted the weapons, the men on the plane didn't want to kill themselves, and Midnight Delta wanted the shot. Yep, nothing to do but chat and wait.

"So, you never told me, how's life as a father?" Clint asked again.

Well this was getting ridiculous, Drake thought. Chatting about who was behind the gun running was one thing.

"Clint, why haven't you and Lydia set a date?" Drake asked.

"Well that concludes the get-to-know-you part of our conversation," Jack said with an uneasy laugh.

"What are you talking about, I want to know, too," Dare said.

"Quiet," Finn commanded. "Yemisi is saying something. Can any of you on the ground hear him?"

"I got him," Dare said. "He's saying that as soon as the weapons are loaded, he'll make the transfer to their account. M-16 boy is saying half now. The rest when the weapons are loaded."

"You've got your orders. No shots taken until Finn takes out the American. Then I want everyone else taken out but Yemisi, and I want the tires on the jeeps useless. Are we set?" Mason asked.

Everyone said yes. They waited. Yemisi waved his men to start the unloading process, and the man holding the M-16 stepped forward and to the right as he waved them through. Blood and bone sprayed out as Finn took a head shot. Bullets rang out, only slightly muffled by the rain.

Drake, took aim. Again, and again. Until he saw that there was not another man standing.

"Report!" Mason demanded.

"Fine," Dare said. "But I'm on the move. Yemisi took off like a bat out of hell."

"Good," Clint's voice was clear as a bell.

"Fine," Jack drawled.

"I'm good," Finn said.

"Good," Drake reported.

"The pilot?" Clint asked.

"He and the co-pilot were in my line of sight. I got them," Jack said.

"I want that plane and weapons destroyed. Jack, you and Drake follow Dare. We'll catch up."

"Roger that."

YEMISI MIGHT HAVE STARTED out like a bat out of hell, but he sure slowed down fast. Turned out that besides the radio in the jeep the man had a satellite phone. Dare overheard him making a call to his brother.

"His brother said he didn't have anyone to send for him. He was stuck on his own. Sounded like a power play. Now that Yemisi lost his men and the weapons, he's low man on the totem pole."

"Did he say how far it was to meet up with him?"

"About four days hike, if he was in good shape,"

Drake let out a low laugh. Dare's eyes glittered with laughter in the dark. "Like I said, typical brother bullshit. Kind of like the stuff you were slinging Clint's way."

"I wasn't making him schlep through the jungle for four days."

All hint of laughter left Dare's eyes. "Yeah, well, he was promising him a reward when he got there." Dare's voice dripped with despair. "We've got to get those girls out of there."

Bile rose in Drake's throat. He looked at Jack who stared off into the distance, his face a mask of thunder.

"Anyway, he's going to sleep for the night. So the others have time to catch up," Dare said.

Jack finally looked over at them. "And another thing that's makin' me sick is that it's Americans supplying the Boko Haram with weapons."

Drake took his meaning. He knew a little bit of Jack's wife's story, and these young orphan's plight had to be hitting him especially hard. No wonder he was focusing on the weapons.

"Tell me about the Decault Group," Drake prompted. "What happened in Costa Rica?"

"We took 'em out. All but the pilot, he got away. Mason

thinks they had some inside intel." Hell, Jack's Texas accent was on steroids. Yep, he was really upset.

"Mason thinks there was a mole?"

"That's what he told Captain Hale. It was a close call."

Drake turned to Dare, and the dark-haired man nodded his head solemnly. "Something was definitely fishy. They almost expected us. The pilot never turned off the engines. They had the same set up with the trigger that time I took the shot after the weapons were unloaded."

Drake's mind raced a mile a minute. He kept circling back to that weasel Edwin Marsh who kept insisting this was not going to be the drop site for the weapons. He wasn't just a weasel, there had been a sick that just oozed off the bastard.

"Mase?" Drake said into the headset. When he didn't answer, he called out Clint's name.

They were still out of range.

"What?" Dare asked.

He could see Jack's blond eyebrow raise.

"Marsh. I think he might be dirty. If there was somebody giving information on the Costa Rica op, then it's possible there was for this one too. My money's on Edwin Marsh, the slimy little fuck," Drake said.

Both men nodded in agreement. Jack's grin was positively feral.

"I want him. He's mine. I remember what he said about those girls. I'm personally taking that boy out." Again, Jack's drawl was thick.

"I think you'll have to stand in line," Dare said as he clapped the big Texan on the shoulder.

"Riled much?" Drake asked trying to dispel Jack's anger.

"Don't," Jack bit out. "Don't make light of this. I know you're trying to get me to loosen up, but some things won't stand, treason and the atrocities being visited on those poor young girls are two of those."

"You're right Jack," Drake said softly. "You're absolutely right."

They waited in silence for the rest of the team to catch up, and watched over Yemisi who slept. When Mason arrived, Drake told him his suspicions.

"Clint, call Sheila. I think Drake's instincts are spot on."

Clint nodded. After he was done with the call, he swore a blue streak. Mason finally cut him off. "Just tell us," he said with a sigh.

"Marsh is in the wind," Clint said.

"Are they looking for him?" Finn asked.

"Yeah, but not too hard. Now they're going to step it up," Clint answered. "But Sheila's going to be pulling threads to see who he could have been working with who would have known about the Costa Rica operation as well. She was actually pretty excited about the news."

"Well goody for her," Jack said sarcastically.

Every man stared at him. That was completely out of character.

"Jack, are you all right?" Mason asked.

"Yeah," Jack said tightly. "This Yemisi just needs to get his ass in gear. Mason, do you have any idea as to how we're going to rescue these girls?"

"Same as always, we wait for an opportunity to present itself, then depend on Finn to pull a miracle out of his ass."

It was true. How often had Finn come up with something they needed at just the right time? Hell, the man was fucking MacGyver.

"But here's my rabbit out of the hat. As soon as the rain lets up a little bit, a chopper will be bringing in Gray and his team. They'll follow our coordinates and meet up with us.

His team was just as adamant that those girls needed rescuing."

Drake was relieved to see Jack's face lose some of its strain.

"That's good news," Jack finally said.

AT LEAST THE rain had let up. Clint was in a better mood. But now it was hot, muggy, and buggy. Thank God for the insect repellent. Further on the con side was Drake in the rear with Wyatt Leeds, the youngest member of the two teams, and the kid thought he was funny. He wasn't.

"Didn't Dex just tell me that you had a kid? That's really cool. Girl or boy?"

Drake rolled his eyes. "Boy."

"Is this the first time you left him?" Wyatt asked as they both vaulted over a log.

"Yes." Drake was hoping that answering in monosyllables would get the point across to Wyatt that he wasn't interested in carrying on a conversation.

"That must have been tough. What's the little guy's name?"

"Andrew."

"I have a cousin named Andrew. Hope your kid doesn't turn out like him. He was in juvie a lot. Bet he ends up in prison."

Drake shuddered at the thought of prison, since both of his parents were currently incarcerated. Really, he needed to get this kid to shut up.

"For the love of God, Wyatt, I can't hear myself think, just give it a rest for a while, will ya?"

"Sure thing." Wyatt grinned easily. Drake got the feeling Wyatt was told to shut up pretty often.

They'd been following Yemisi for three and a half days. Jack and Hunter Diaz were on point a couple of clicks ahead of them, scoping out the terrain. Both teams were antsy to find the girls. Meanwhile, Clint had been in touch with Sheila. She said that Edwin Marsh's body was found in Brussels. Apparently, someone had not been happy with the fact that the weapons sale had not gone through as planned. As far as Drake was concerned, it couldn't have happened to a nicer guy.

"Got something," Jack's voice came through Drake's headset.

Drake and Wyatt paused as they waited for Jack to continue. He was taking forever. The two of them started moving again, and then after twenty minutes, they heard muted sounds and Jack spoke. "We found two of the girls. Hunter is speaking to them in French. They escaped. We need a medic."

Gray came on the line, "Aiden, go up ahead and help."

Drake knew his brother-in-law was the medic for Black Dawn. They had a problem though. They needed to get the girls treated, but still allow Yemisi to move forward toward his brother's encampment without seeing the SEALs and the girls who'd escaped.

"I'm sticking like glue to Yemisi," Mason said. "He's heading northwest. You head southeast with the girls, and watch my GPS signal so we don't meet. We should be fine."

"Roger that," Jack said.

"We might not have to do that," Hunter said over the com link.

"Why?" Mason asked.

"The girls want to take us back to where the others are being held. We could just eliminate Yemisi right now."

There was silence.

"How reliable are they?" Mason finally asked. "Will they get lost?"

"Even if they get lost, their trail will be easy enough to track. We've got this," Jack assured him.

There was dead air on the com. Two minutes later Mason said, "It's done. We don't have to worry about Yemisi anymore. Everybody let's move onto Jack and Hunter's coordinates. I want to have rescued those girls by morning."

Jack was picking up one of the girls when Drake and Wyatt caught up to them. The young girl was tall, but she was thin and hunched over, obviously in pain. His heart went out to her. The other girl was smaller. She had a grim smile on her face as she looked up at the men circling her. She spoke to Hunter and Aiden excitedly.

With no hint of fear, she pushed past Drake and started walking. "What did she say?" Drake asked Aiden.

"She said that we were big and strong, and our guns were bigger than the men who had held her captive. She expects us to kill all the bad men *tout suite*."

"What does that mean?" Wyatt asked.

"Pretty damn quick," Aiden answered with a laugh. "We just got our marching orders from a teenage girl. I love it."

"That's because you're used to taking them from Evie, who isn't much bigger than this girl is." Drake grinned. He had to find something good in all of this, and that girl's spirit was something bright to hold onto. Thinking about the girl who was being held so gently by Jack hurt his heart. But this one was a soul sister of Evie and made his heart clench. He needed to protect her, just as he had always needed to protect his six younger sisters.

Drake watched as Hunter caught up with the girl whose name was Elise, and squatted in front of her. She listened solemnly, and then he got up and the two of them headed toward the rest of the team.

"You explained?" Mason asked.

"Yeah, I told her that she would be staying here with me, and the rest of you would follow her and Isobel's trail. She said we needed to hurry back or she would run away and come help us."

Every single SEAL had to work hard to keep a straight face. Yes, she was definitely Evie's African twin.

"You better keep a good watch on her then," Gray told his man.

"You better believe it," Hunter said. "I asked her not to make me look bad in front of my commander."

Drake turned one last time to look at Jack holding the injured girl Isobel, as Elise paced in front of them. God, Drake hoped that all the girls were in such good shape as Elise, but he knew there wasn't a chance in hell of that being true, it was likely they were more like Isobel. He thought back to the prayers he'd said for Karen when she'd been clinging to life, and said some more now.

7

"You're going to be fine, Andrew, the doctor said so." She kissed Andrew's forehead, and reassured herself that he didn't have a fever as she wrapped him up warmly in a tiny little leather bomber jacket that Mason and Sophia had bought for him. Then Karen wrapped him in his soft baby blanket and picked him up.

"Are you ready for a walk?" It seemed counterintuitive that she would be taking her sick son outside, but the doctor had assured her that for the croup a ten-minute walk out in the cool air would be good for his lungs.

Andrew looked up at her and started coughing. It sounded so agonizing. The cough went on and on, it sounded like he was barking. *It's just a mild case of the croup, the doctor had said.* Karen fought back the tears. She wished Drake were there. Suck it up, Eastman, how many kindergartners did you used to teach? How many of them were sick at times? Didn't you cope?

Her phone rang, it was her mom. She put her ear buds in as she headed out the door. "How's Andy?"

"Andrew," Karen automatically corrected. "He sounds

terrible, Mom." Karen placed the phone between her and the baby as she locked her apartment and headed down the walkway. The sun was just setting. She saw Mr. Ortiz walking his dog and he waved to her.

Karen rocked Andrew as he continued to cough. God, she hated the word croup, it sounded like a disease from the middle ages. "What, Mom?" She hadn't been listening.

"Honey, he's sounding better."

Every cough had felt like a blow, so Karen had missed the fact that the amount and severity of coughing had begun to decrease.

She looked down at her son's pink cheeks. "Are you feeling better, sweet boy?" He gave a soft cough. She laughed. "I'll take that as a yes." She looked at the phone. They'd been out for eight minutes. "The doctor was right, Mom."

"They often are, Honey."

"He's doing better."

"I hear that."

Her hand trembled as she tried to insert the key in the lock. She was so tired and relieved. As soon as she got into the apartment she locked the door and dropped onto the couch. Andrew let out a tired whimper.

"Are you doing okay, Karen? Do I need to come back down? Where's Piper?"

"She worked with a friend over the weekend."

"Why would she have done that?" Her mother's tone was clipped.

"She didn't know Andrew was sick," she defended Drake's young sister. "Seriously, Mom, I'm fine. Andrew and I just need a nap."

"When was the last time you slept?"

Karen rested her head against the back of the couch and

unwrapped the blanket from around Andrew as he wiggled. "I'm getting my zees."

"Bullshit."

"Mom, you had four kids, you did this just fine."

"Your dad came home every night, I wasn't cut open, I wasn't trying to plan a wedding or move into a new home."

Karen sat up straighter. Her mother couldn't possibly know about the fact that she was moving out of the apartment this week, could she? She'd be down here in a shot if she'd found out.

"Karen Marie, why aren't you answering me? Your silence sounds guilty."

"Okay, you're right I'm not getting as much sleep as I would like."

"I worry about you. Have you heard when Drake's coming home?" Karen's heart plunged. There had been no word for the last thirteen days. She hated these types of missions the most. Usually they got *some* word.

Andrew started coughing again. "Mom, Andrew needs to be changed, can we talk about this later?"

"Only if you promise to call me later. If you don't, I'll start stalking you. Are we clear?"

"Crystal."

"I love you, baby."

"I know you do, Mom. I love you too," she said right before she hung up.

Slowly Karen picked up Andrew and walked down the hall to her bedroom, he coughed the entire way. Even through his jacket she could feel his chest wheezing and it was scary. She'd just been at the pediatrician's office yesterday, he'd assured her that her boy was going to be fine, but he sounded horrible. She put him down on the bed and took off his clothes so she could change his diaper and Karen crooned to him.

"You're going to be big and strong like your daddy, did you know that? You're probably going to be stubborn and a smartass, and make me laugh. But don't think just because you're cute you'll get away with things like your daddy does. I'm going to be watching you."

Andrew's coughing slowed as he listened to her voice. "Do I just need to keep talking to you all night, and then you'll get better?"

He wheezed in response.

"Keep it together, Karen," she said in the same singsong voice. She didn't want to upset her baby, so even when she wanted to rant and rave, she kept her tone soothing. "The doctor said lots of babies get the croup, and this is not a big deal. Mom said I had it too." She watched in horror as a tear splashed on Andrew's belly. She quickly wiped it off.

Dammit, she needed to keep it together. She got his clean diaper on and picked him up. He started coughing. She didn't have the strength to walk with him. She could only sit on the bed and rock him.

Eventually his coughing turned to crying and Karen realized she'd zoned out. It was time for his dinner. She got settled and in between coughs, he fed.

"Karen?" She heard Piper call as she came in the front door of the apartment.

She sat up straighter, and put a big smile on her face. She didn't want Piper to worry.

"Back here," Karen responded.

Andrew let out a cry, that turned into a barking cough.

Piper hurried into the master bedroom. She looked down at her nephew in concern. "What's wrong with Andrew?"

"It's just the croup," Karen said blithely.

"Bella used to get that, and Trenda would go crazy with worry. How are you holding up? Why didn't you call me? I wouldn't have stayed with Jan over the weekend, I would have been here."

"You guys were working on your biology project. You wanted to get an A. I was fine."

Piper scowled as she sat down on the side of the bed. "Did you call anyone to come and help you? Evie? Sophia? Lydia? Anyone?"

"Piper, the croup is normal. I took him to the pediatrician, they assured me he was fine, all is good." She smiled. "I was waiting for you to come home so I could tell you some fantastic news."

"First tell me how you got to the pediatrician. You're not supposed to be driving."

"I took a taxi."

"Why would you do that, when you could have called Evie or me?"

"I didn't want to bother anyone."

"That's stupid."

"No it's not. I can take care of myself," Karen protested. "No let me tell you my good news."

Piper arched her eyebrow. God, she looked just like her big brother when she did that.

"Tell me."

"Mr. Albertson, the landlord, came and talked to me. He offered me a bonus if we moved out early."

Piper started shaking her head before Karen could even finished her sentence.

"It was a sizeable bonus."

"I don't care how big the bonus is. There is enough going on with you still recovering, Drake gone, the wedding, and now Andrew being sick. You don't need to move into the townhome any sooner than you planned to."

"In my defense, he offered it before Andrew got sick."

"You only get half points taken off. It's still a stupid move."

Karen's auburn hair sifted over Andrew's face as she nodded her head. He grabbed a fistful as he continued to suck.

Piper left the room, then came back. "I thought I saw them, but I didn't believe it. There are boxes in the living room. You've been packing. Are you out of your mind? Karen, you're doing too much."

"I wasn't until Andrew got sick. Seriously Piper I was handling everything just fine until Andrew got the croup."

She'd screwed up. Plain and simple. But she would work her way out of this mess. She always did. If she just weren't so damned tired everything would be just fine. It's just that there were calls all the time trying to find a caterer and a band, and all she wanted to do was bond with Andrew. That had been her big plan, and it was crumbling right before her eyes.

"What you need to do is take care of yourself and Andrew."

"I will. I am." It was clear that Andrew was done feeding.

"Hand him to me." Piper held out her arms. Karen handed her son to the young woman. He immediately started whimpering, then coughing. Piper got up. "I'm going to walk around the apartment with him for a while. Bella always liked when we did that. Why don't you rest?"

"I'm fine, I think I'll go make some dinner."

"I've got dinner, you nap."

"I'm not tired," Karen insisted.

"I mean this in the nicest, most respectful way," Piper

said as she jostled her nephew on her shoulder. "You look like crap on a cracker. Go to sleep."

Karen stared at Piper in surprise. The girl she'd met two years ago would never had said that to her. But then again, now they were family, what was more, she probably did look like shit. "Okay, I'll take a quick nap, but wake me in a half hour, okay?"

"I hear you," Piper said.

KAREN WOKE WITH A START. She didn't hear a sound. Her heart started beating a million miles a minute. Where was Andrew? Why wasn't he coughing? What time was it? She threw back the covers and vaulted out of bed. It was ten o'clock at night, three hours since she had gone to sleep. She ran down the darkened hallway to Piper's room. It was empty. When she skidded into the living room she tripped over one of the boxes she'd packed, and she went flying into the arm of the couch, rolling sideways and then slamming her head into the corner of the coffee table. She couldn't breathe, nor could she move for long moments. The pain in her head was intense.

But worse than the ache in her head, was not knowing where Andrew was. She started calling out Piper's name. No answer.

She pushed herself up from the floor, tenderly touching the back of her head, she could already feel the bump forming. She aimed for the hallway, but almost crashed into the wall. Righting herself, she did her best to head toward her room, where her cell phone was. She needed to find Piper. As she passed the bathroom in the hallway she saw the light on underneath the door and heard the water running, she pushed the door open. The room was steamy, and Piper was holding a quiet and smiling Andrew in her arms.

"I did an internet search. Google said steam would help his cough."

Karen sagged against the doorframe gasping for breath.

"Steam's good," Karen whispered as she took one step into the bathroom. It was all she could manage as she slipped down the side of the wall.

"Karen?"

Piper's voice came from a long way away.

"Karen, answer me, right this minute."

She sounded bossy like Drake did.

Andrew was coughing again, but then she didn't hear him. Where'd they go? She thought she heard Piper yelling. Who was she yelling at? It didn't matter. It felt good in the warm bathroom. She just needed to rest here for a while. But her head hurt. A lot. Maybe if she just got down on the floor. Oh, she was on the floor. Maybe she needed to curl up. She pulled her knees up to her tummy, and curling her arms around her aching head. Yeah, that was better.

"Oh God, she's in the fetal position. Come quick!"

"Who ya talkin' too?" Was that her slurred voice?

"Honey, just rest, the ambulance will be here any minute," Piper said. She heard Andrew coughing.

She really hurt. It reminded her of being in the delivery room. She wanted Drake. Drake would make it better if he were here.

IT WAS three o'clock in the morning, the best time for an attack. This time the guards were awake and alert, not that it mattered. They were dispatched quickly by Dalton Sullivan of Black Dawn and Dare. Then Finn, Jack, and Hunter took position up in trees, while the rest of the teams headed into the encampment.

Many of the girls were tied by their necks to a tree. A few were stuck in pallets on the ground with one terrorist or another. Drake forced himself not to think about it and instead focus on the mission.

Almost everyone in the camp was asleep, which would make the op easy. Stealth was the SEALs bread and butter. Mason took point as the leader, and he indicated that the men who slept solo were the first ones who needed to be quietly killed. There were seven. If anyone raised the alarm, that's when the snipers would be deployed.

Drake had just finished his target, when he heard a girl scream.

Fuck!

A shot rang out at the same time he felt a bug bite his arm. It was a big bug.

Shit, fuck, piss, he'd been shot again. He hated getting shot.

He hunkered down and took aim at his next target, but it was too late, one of the sniper's got him before he had a chance. Where was the fun in that?

To his left a girl started screaming and crying. He saw a man with a gun to her chin. It was pressed in deep. The guy was wild-eyed, his finger was close to pulling. Drake stood up and waved his arms. "Don't shoot," he warned his team members.

He heard crying around him. There hadn't been that many Boko Haram in the camp, he had to assume his team had taken the rest out, and this was the last bastard left. The man started babbling in French. Where was Aiden?

"He wants us to let him go on one of the trucks," Aiden said from behind him.

"Fine," Mason said. "Promise it to him. We'll get a shot by then. Got it men?"

All snipers answered in the affirmative.

As Aiden and Mason arranged for the soon-to-be dead man's truck, Drake turned his attention to the girls who had all huddled together near the tree.

"*Parlais vous Anglais*?" Wyatt asked. The crying just got worse. Wyatt kept at it.

"Put a sock in it Leeds," Gray commanded.

Gray crouched down in front of one of the girls who was already trying to undo the rope around her neck and started talking soothingly to her. His blond and gray hair glinted in the early morning light. She stared at it. He pulled out his knife and she shrank back.

A shot rang out, and a girl screamed.

"Goddammit." Gray muttered. They all waited long moments, and finally a girl, covered in blood, walked over with Aiden.

"Thank God, you can talk to them in French," Gray said. "Tell them we want to cut the ropes off them."

Aiden nodded and started talking in French. Girls started speaking all at once, until he let out a long whistle. Drake might not understand French, but he knew the next words out of Aiden's mouth were, "One at a time." Aiden held up his knife. A girl held up her hand. He waded through the throng and got to her. He cut off the rope tethering her to the tree, then once again they all started shouting at the same time. That was their signal to start cutting them loose.

Drake assessed them and instead of helping, he went out to the camp and found what blankets he could and started cutting them up so that he had some wraps for the girls who were missing clothes. He needed to do this for his own peace of mind or he would start cutting up the corpses of the men into tiny little bits.

What kind of animals had these men been? They were just young girls.

When he started handing out bits of blankets, he was met with pathetic amounts of gratitude.

He saw Clint standing off to the side and double timed it over to him. "So what's the good word?"

"We're about forty kilometers from their orphanage. Parts of it was burned but there's an international outcry for the safe return of the girls, so that's good. People are helping to get it set to rights."

"Are people going to meet up with us to bring them back?"

"That's the plan. Probably five miles out there's a good road, and there'll be trucks to bring them back to their town."

"Will they have the facilities to help them?" Drake asked as he looked at the girls. He could see some of them already had the hundred-yard stare that was normally reserved for men who had seen too much combat.

Clint looked at him with compassion. "Drake, I know that trust comes hard to you, but we did our part, we have to assume that the civilians will do their part."

"Have you called Hunter?"

"Yeah, he's on his way. He's says that Isobel is doing better, she can walk if some of the others need to be carried."

"Yeah, they'll need to be carried." This time Drake assessed Clint. Clint saw it.

"I'm going to be fine. Lydia's good, so I'm good."

"Well, if anybody is capable of carrying females through the jungle, it's you." Drake attempted to tease, but it fell flat.

"Fuck you, Avery," Clint said with a half grin.

"Just saying."

AFTER FIVE CLICKS, Mason and Gray called a halt to the happy little hike. Elise looked like she was ready to fall over. She had actually carried one of the other girls on her back from time to time. Drake was continually amazed by her fortitude.

The girls that could, were carrying the supplies that they had foraged from the camp. Hunter worked with some of the older girls to get everybody fed. This helped to keep morale up by giving them something to do. But still, there was a lot of crying.

Elise came over to where Drake was sitting. "You are big," she said in halting English.

"*Oui*," Drake said yes in French. Elise clapped her hands in delight then started quickly speaking torrents of French.

"Whoa, whoa, whoa. I can't understand. I can say *oui* and *merci*. That's it," Drake explained.

"You are big man."

"I got that." He smiled.

"You are hurt," she pointed to the bandage on his bicep. Last thing he needed was an infection in the jungle, but still it was nothing.

"It doesn't hurt."

"You save us."

"My team did."

"We go home. Reverend Mother, she hurt too."

"Did the men hurt her?"

Elise nodded.

The animals.

"They kill Father Thomas. Isobel talk me." Elise's eyes filled with tears.

Damn.

Drake kept his words simple. "There will be many more people at the orphanage. They will help." He looked at the other girls. One was in really bad shape. Aiden and Finn were doing everything they could to get her the care she needed. Aiden had carried her all day.

"Far time?"

Drake looked at Elise and tried to think what she was asking. "I don't understand."

"Many mornings?"

He finally got it. He held up three fingers. "Three mornings."

She nodded. He put his palms together and put them under his tilted head and made a snoring sound. She giggled. "Sleep now," he said. She got up and joined the other girls.

"She's a kick," Dare said as he sat down next to Drake.

"I don't know how the hell she's keeping it together."

"Charlotte would too," Dare said referring to the teenage girl he was helping to raise. "Hell, so would your sisters."

"At least until the crisis was over with," Drake said softly. He thought about his sister, Chloe.

"But then someone will be there to help them. Right?"

Drake thought about it, and knew that Dare was correct. Chloe was now happy and healthy. With the right help these girls could be as well.

"I'm going to take the first watch," Drake said as he stood up.

IT WAS a somber group that reached the trucks three days later. The girl who had been so badly injured had died the day before. When they arrived in Amoto the girls were swarmed by villagers, aid workers, and members of the international press.

Drake watched as Hunter and Aiden both took time to hug and reassure Elise. Boy, that girl had wormed her way into everyone's heart, but there was just no real time for protracted good-byes, they had to get the hell out of there.

As they were taking the last of the injured girls into the clinic, Mason and Drake's pictures were taken. The photographer had run away as soon as he had done it and disappeared into the crowd of reporters. Mason was pissed. Hopefully with all the dirt, sweat, and beards they'd be unrecognizable. As soon as it happened, Gray confiscated an empty truck and got the two SEAL teams the hell out of town.

"Clint. Dex. What's the ETA on the choppers? Where are they landing?" Gray yelled over his shoulder as he drove down the dirt road.

"They'll be here in less than an hour. Keep going down this road for another two kilometers."

Drake was relieved to see nobody was following them. Thank God, the story was the girl's return. They ended up waiting for almost an hour by the time they heard the choppers. Mason was motionless after they got strapped in.

"It's going to be okay." Drake smiled. "We look like the guys on Duck Dynasty."

Mason didn't crack a smile, instead he turned to Clint. "Radio it in. I know it's the middle of the night back home, tell whoever is on duty that we need to talk to Captain Hale when we can."

"Drake's right. You two are going to be hard to recognize," Clint assured him.

"We're white. We're in fatigues. Everybody is going to assume we're Americans. We have a fucking problem," Mason bit out.

Clint took a deep breath and went up to the front of the helicopter to the communications center.

"Mase—"

"Drake, I don't want to hear it."

Drake looked over at Finn who gave a small shake of his head. Mason was right. This was probably going to go viral. They were supposed to stay under the radar. What was more, their mission had been to take out the weapons dealers, not save the orphans. That had been outside their purview. God knows how the suits were going to react.

Clint came back and strapped himself in. "They said he'll be available by the time we reach the Margaret Ekpo Airport."

Mason gave a sharp nod.

Drake hoped it wasn't going to be as bad as Mason thought.

SHEILA MET them as soon as they arrived. Her grim look said it all.

"I take it we've made the news already?" Gray said.

"Not you," she said. She pointed at Drake and at Mason. "Him and him. Clear as day. The Associated Press is already trying to figure out if it is Delta Force or Navy SEALs."

"That doesn't seem fair to the Green Berets, now does it?" Wyatt said.

"What he said," Drake agreed.

"What did I say on the chopper, Avery?" Mason growled.

Shit, Mason was well and truly pissed. As a matter of fact, Drake could never remember him being this angry. Drake breathed deeply. He knew the real issue, and he hadn't wanted to think about it. It was the facial recognition software that was out there. Mason's eyes glittered as he stared at him. Drake nodded. Yep, this wasn't good.

"Let's see the pics, Sheila." Mason held out his hand. She handed over her cell phone. Drake leaned over to look.

"Well, it could have been worse," Mason said resignedly. "Has Captain Hale called?"

"Twice," she answered. "You can take it in private. Well, the two of you can," she said looking at Gray Tyler. The two men followed her to the small office that butted up to the conference room.

Clint, Dare, Finn, and Jack, all gathered around Drake. Sheila had left her cell phone with him.

"You don't look like the Duck Dynasty dude, you look like bigfoot," Clint joked.

"Nah, bigfoot's more handsome," Dare said patting Drake on the back.

They were right. The problem was going to be that Americans were where they weren't supposed to be.

"Drake, come in here."

Ah fuck. Obviously, he'd thought he was in the clear too soon. He turned and saw Mason staring at him, but he wasn't looking as mad as he had been. He looked really concerned. Now what? Drake went into the office as Gray and Sheila exited.

"Yeah?"

"Andrew and Karen are fine. But Karen's had a setback. Nothing serious."

Drake stared at Mason. He knew his friend backward and forward. Mason wouldn't lie to him. Andrew and Karen were alive and safe. That was what was important. His boy. His woman. They were safe.

"What happened?"

"Karen's in the hospital. She's supposed to be discharged in a day or two, so everything's good."

His knees turned to water. Karen was in the hospital?

"You with me big guy?" Mason had his hand on his shoulder.

He needed to be home now. Now. *Now. Now!*

"Drake, talk to me."

"I'm fine."

Mason opened the door to the tiny office. "Need an ETA on a plane home. Now!"

Drake stared at the piss green paint on the wall and waited for the answer, imagining the worst. All he could see was Karen white as a sheet the way she'd been in the delivery room. Please God, don't take her away from me. He shut his eyes. Mason wouldn't lie. But the suits might.

His eyes darted to Mason, then they shot to the door as Dex came in.

"There's a plane heading home in four hours," Dex said.

"Make it sooner. I don't care what you have to do, we need Drake on a plane home in the next half hour, got it?" Mason said grimly.

Drake turned back to study the wall. Now he took note of all the places the paint was peeling, saying prayers in his head at the same time.

Drake waited.

"Captain Hale would give it to us straight," Mason said quietly. Once again, he'd read Drake's mind.

"Did you call Sophia?" Drake asked, turning around to look at his friend.

"The circuits are busy. Aiden's trying to get ahold of Evie with the satellite phone." Drake nodded. He knew they'd tell him if they knew something. Anything. Knowing Evie was with Karen gave him some comfort. Piper too. But Evie...

"Mase? Do you think Captain Hale will approve a first-class ticket?" Clint asked as he rushed into the little room.

"Fuck yeah," Mason said decisively.

"Good, because I've already booked him a seat," Clint said. "Now we've got thirty minutes to get him on the plane." Clint turned to Drake. "Let's get you cleaned up a little so you don't scare the civilians."

Like Drake gave a shit, the only thing that mattered was getting home to Karen. He should have never left her. He should have never left.

8

It was like she was under water. She couldn't make her eyes open. She swore she could hear Andrew crying, but she couldn't get to him.

"Andrew?" That didn't sound like her voice. She tried to open her eyes, but her eyelids felt too heavy. Where was she?

"Karen? It's all right. Don't move. Andrew's right here."

It was Piper. Or was it Evie? They both sounded alike. Why was she so confused?

"Give me Andrew," she slurred.

"Karen, you can't hold him right now. You've got an IV in your arm. Can you open your eyes, Honey? If you open your eyes you can see him."

Andrew started coughing. He sounded just like he had before Piper had taken him into the bathroom. "He needs more steam," Karen said weakly.

"He's doing much better. We had a doctor check him out since we're in the hospital."

"Hospital?" That was Evie talking. Had she said hospital? What were they doing in a hospital? Karen was able to open her eyes a little, and in the dim light she saw Evie and Piper standing beside her bed. Evie was holding Andrew. He looked okay, but then he started to cough.

"Give him to me," she commanded.

"You can't even lift your arms. You're not getting him," Evie said imperiously.

Karen tried to lift her torso off the bed, but everything hurt. "What's wrong with me?"

"You fell. Don't you remember?" Piper asked.

"No," Karen said. Then she remembered the box and the couch, and she nodded. "I remember. But why am I in the hospital, that doesn't make any sense."

"Sure, it makes sense," Evie said vehemently. She bent low and looked at Karen, her eyes blazing. "You don't ask for help. You ran yourself ragged. You were dehydrated, exhausted and you gave yourself a concussion when you fell. You're grounded." Karen tried to lift her arm, so she could touch Andrew, but failed.

"If you tell me you learned your lesson, I'll lay Andrew down beside you for a moment," Evie said. She still sounded pissed.

"I'm sorry." Karen's lower lip trembled. She was sorry. She never meant to do anything to endanger her son.

"Karen, don't cry." Piper pushed Evie to the side. "Evie doesn't mean to be so angry, she was just scared is all. She freaked when I called and told her that you needed an ambulance."

Karen looked at Piper who was nineteen and Evie who was in her mid-twenties and realized that both women had been scared. But despite Piper's words, Evie was well and truly pissed, which hurt, but it also made Karen mad. Talk about the pot calling the kettle black.

"Evie, I don't need a lecture. Give me my son," Karen said with as much quiet dignity as she could summon.

"You do too need a lecture."

"Give me Andrew," Karen said in her best school teacher tone. Which wasn't all that great considering the fact that her throat was dry, and her head felt like a bass drum was beating inside it.

"I'll set him down beside you," Evie acquiesced.

As soon as her son's little body was next to her, despite his coughing, Karen felt soothed. "Are you sure the doctor said he was getting better?" she asked the women.

"Yes," Piper assured her. "Now we just have to get you well."

"When can I leave?"

"They want to keep you under observation for two more days. Then it's bedrest for you."

"For a concussion? That's ridiculous." Why did her voice sound so weak?

"How about for a concussion and exhaustion? You're my sister. I told you, you're grounded."

"Evie, you sound like Drake, and that's not a compliment."

Evie's whole body shuddered. "You could have died," she said softy. "I don't care if I sound like Drake, if I sound like Elvis, or if I sound like my evil mom. Whatever it takes to get through to you that you can't die. I love you too much."

She was standing stiff and straight. "Come here."

Evie shook her head.

"I desperately need a hug," Karen coaxed.

She had to wait four long heartbeats and then Evie rushed over and gently embraced her. "I promise to take care of myself, okay?"

"Thank God."

But seriously, how could she get everything done? She still hadn't found a caterer, or a band. There was the apartment. And if it weren't for wanting to give Drake the wedding he deserved, she throw in the towel, because dammit, she just wanted to spend time with Andrew.

"Karen? Did you hear me?"

Karen tried to clear her head, and she focused on Evie. "What did you say? I missed it."

"You look upset. It's all going to be fine. Piper told me about you needing to move. We've got you covered. I talked to the girls, and we'll have you packed and moved in time. You're coming over to my house to rest."

"I wanted to get Andrew's room ready for him at the townhome. I had it all planned." Her voice trailed off. She wanted to decorate it with white and orange striped curtains, and little helmet decals on the crib. She was painting the room white, but the helmets were going to be orange, the color of the University of Tennessee Volunteers. She even found a baby bib that said, 'Excuse the Spit Up, I Thought I Saw a 'Bama Fan.'

"Honey, you can take care of that after you move in."

"No, it has to be perfect before we get there."

Evie rolled her eyes. "No, it doesn't. You're not thinking straight. This is exactly what landed you in the hospital in the first place. Can you see that?"

Karen looked at Evie. Evie wasn't mad at her; this time it was like she was trying to explain something important. But it still wasn't computing.

"But Evie, Drake would be able to get it all done."

"Fuck Karen, he would have bought his friends pizza and beer, and probably sat on his ass directing traffic."

"That's not true and you know it. He does so much. Look how he sacrificed for all of you for over a decade. Look at the life he leads as a SEAL. I want to be just as strong. He needs someone who can take care of him." Once again, her voice trailed off, and she had trouble keeping her eyes open. She felt someone pick up Andrew, who seemed to be sleeping, thank the Lord. She was relieved he wasn't coughing.

She felt someone press a kiss against her forehead. "You're a nut. Can't you see that you're perfect for him?" Evie whispered.

She heard the door close and she wished it were true. She wished she were good enough.

IT WAS déjà vu all over again. He frantically asked at the nurse's station what room Karen Eastman was in. It seemed to take the nurse hours to answer his question. Finally, she told him, and he literally ran down the hall, ignoring all of the glares.

He stopped short of banging the door open, because he didn't want to scare her, or wake her, or some such shit. Instead, he took a long breath and eased the door open slowly. She was a small mound under a thin blanket. When had his curvaceous woman gotten so slim? For fuck's sake, she'd just had a baby.

He walked silently across the floor and looked down at her, not missing anything. She was pale, her auburn lashes showed starkly against her translucent skin. Her cheeks were hollowed out. They hadn't been when he'd left her sixteen days ago. Her hand was clenching the blanket so tightly her knuckles were white, so even now she wasn't relaxed. She was either stressed or scared beyond her limits. He cupped her jaw and placed a soft kiss on her dry lips.

Her eyes fluttered open, but she didn't focus. Instead of being happy, she looked forlorn.

"Aren't you glad to see me?" he asked quietly. Desperately. Please say he hadn't lost her. Please say she would forgive him for leaving.

She just stared, her eyes welling with tears.

"Karen?"

She slammed her lids shut. "Karen, Honey?" His thumb traced a lazy pattern across her cheek. Hoping to coax her back to him.

She opened her eyes up again, and he saw the warmth in the beautiful green depths. It gave him hope. "Drake, it's really you? I'm not dreaming this time?"

That explained it.

"It's me, Honey."

"I'm in the hospital." She sounded so lost. Another thing that wasn't his Karen.

"Not for much longer," he assured her. "I'm busting you out today."

"Really?" Karen pushed up onto her elbows.

"I promise."

She searched his face. He had no idea what she was looking for, so he did what he always did. He said what was in his heart. "I love you."

"I love you more," she whispered back. Tears formed.

"Hey, what's going on? Except the fact that I come back, and I see you've worked yourself to a frazzle and you're in the hospital with a concussion, everything's good now, right?"

"I knew you'd be mad at me." Tears started to fall in earnest.

He sat down on the side of the bed and drew her into his arms. "Hey, hey, I'm not mad. Scared shitless, but not mad."

God, that moment when Mason said she was in the hospital ranked up there as one of the worst in his life. He gently rocked and kissed her warm temple while wisps of auburn hair tickled his nose.

"Are you okay now?" He asked after her tears subsided.

"I'm fine. I'm sorry I cried all over you. You know this isn't me. I hate these damned hormones."

"Karen, I fell in love with the non-pregnant Karen, I fell deeper in love with the pregnant Karen and I'm over the moon with the woman who is a mother. I know your body's being hit with a lot of different hormones, but have you ever thought that I'm different too?"

She looked at him in confusion.

"I'm a father now. My instincts where you and Andrew are concerned is off the charts. I've had to learn to rein it in."

Karen let out a quick laugh. "This is you reining it in?"

He looked at her in confusion. "Well yeah."

"You're so pretty." She smiled sweetly at him.

He knew that was their code for he was being a dumbshit, but what was she talking about? He was reining it in. He went on the mission, hadn't he? He hadn't flown Trenda from Tennessee to come watch her, like he obviously should have. Now that he thought about it, reining it in was a stupid fucking idea.

"Well my days of reining it in are over with," he said fiercely.

"What do you mean? You haven't taken it easy in the slightest. As a matter of fact, you've been tyrannical."

"You haven't seen anything yet. From what Evie's been telling me you've been trying to be superwoman."

"Well weren't you the one who called me a Warrior Princess?" she asked tartly.

Drake reared back. "This isn't funny. Jesus Fucking

Christ. You ended up in the goddamn hospital. Piper said you took some sort of bonus from our landlord, so you intended to move out by the end of the week. Andrew's sick. The wedding is two-and-a-half weeks away. You ended up unconscious from a concussion. Do you have any idea how fucking serious that is? You scared years off my life."

She shoved a finger into his chest. "You listen to me you overbearing oaf. I'm more than capable of handling things on my own. Don't you try to dictate to me how to run things when you're on a mission. At least thirty percent of our life is going to be spent this way, and I knew that when I agreed to be with you. The last thing I need is you second guessing me, I had enough of that from three older brothers."

"Well they did a shitty job of getting the point across." Drake glared at her.

"You are not my big brother, you are going to be my husband. My partner. So, don't you try dictating to me you Neanderthal."

Normally Karen was a little subtler in how she dealt with him, but seeing her go head-to-head with him, made him feel a whole hell of a lot better. Seeing her so pale and thin, when he walked in, had him shaking in his shoes. Her yelling made him want to do cartwheels. He grinned.

"Why are you smirking?" she asked suspiciously.

He swooped in for a kiss. A long kiss. Soon it was wet and passionate.

She pushed him away. "Ewww."

"What?" he questioned, perplexed.

"I haven't brushed my teeth."

"You taste like Karen." He bent to take her mouth again.

"I taste like hospital food." She said turning her head.

He put a finger to her cheek and tilted her back. "I like lime jello." This time the kiss was slower, sweeter. Karen wound her arms around his neck. She might be thinner, but her full breasts felt luscious against his chest. Soon they were both breathing heavy. He feathered his kisses to the side of her mouth, her cheek, her neck, until finally they were back under control.

"I missed you so much, Drake. Where's Andrew? God, I should have asked that first thing," she wailed. "I'm a terrible mother."

He saw she was serious. "Hey, don't go overboard. I was in your face, remember. Subconsciously you knew he was safe, otherwise I would have told you differently. Cut yourself some slack, please Baby?"

She bit her lower lip.

"Please?"

She sighed and nodded. "Now tell me where he is."

"He's with my sisters, over at Evie's place."

"How's he doing with the croup?"

"Piper said to tell you he's almost over it. She knew you'd be worried."

"Still I should have—"

"Karen. Okay, that does it. Obviously, you can't lighten up. I'm taking charge."

She scowled at him.

"Come on, let's get you dressed. We're staying over at Evie and Aiden's place while the apartment's getting packed up and moved to the townhome."

"I should—"

"If any phrase but 'I should listen to Drake' comes out of your mouth, we're going to have a problem. You're on lockdown for a week. Doctor's orders."

"Let me talk to the doctor. I heard something about two days, but I sure as hell didn't hear a week." She pushed back the blanket and pushed at Drake, so she could swing her legs out of the bed. "You're in my way."

"Ask nicely, and I'll move."

"Please move, so we can go see our son."

"Now that was nice." He couldn't resist. He kissed her one last time.

———

DRAKE HATED TAKING favors from Aiden O'Malley. Even though he had long ago realized he was a stand-up guy. He still intended to outwardly hold a grudge for at least another year for the way he had treated Evie. It was a brother thing. That's why it was galling that he had to take a favor from him. But Karen needed the best place to rest before they moved into their townhome and that was Aiden and Evie's house.

"What has you frowning?" Karen asked as she adjusted the pillows behind her. Drake swiftly tried to take over the task.

"I can manage this on my own," she slapped away his help. "The doctor said I needed to take it easy, not stay in bed."

"Humor me. Just for today and tomorrow." He poured more than his normal Southern accent into his request.

"I know what you're doing," she groused.

"Is it going to work?" He smiled.

"Yes, dammit, but on one condition."

He cocked an eyebrow.

"You crawl into bed with me. You look tired."

"Honey, I have to—"

"Nope. That's my condition. Take it or leave it." He

looked at her with her hair fanned out across the mound of pillows.

He gave a swift thought to Andrew who was currently holding court with his aunt out in the living room. Karen probably had two more hours before she had to nurse and anything he could do to talk her into a nap he was all for. What was more, holding her close was his favorite pastime in the world. But she was wrong, he wasn't tired.

She must have seen him hesitate. "Drake, please."

"Okay."

He sat next to her and untied his boots, and Karen started to scratch his back.

"Up." She laughed, because she knew what he meant. She lifted his shirt and scratched his bare back. "That feels so damn good."

"You're easy, Avery."

"No, you're just that good, Karen." She played him like a finely tuned instrument. It had to be five minutes before he realized that he still had to take off his socks. "Honey, you have to stop."

"I don't want to. I love touching you."

"I love it to, but if you want me to crawl into bed with you, you have to stop."

He shivered as she scraped both sets of nails down his back, then licked the line of his spine and pulled down his shirt.

"Actually, I don't know why I'm pulling this down, you should take it off."

Drake had his socks off and came around to the other side of the bed in his jeans and T-Shirt. Karen was wearing soft sweat pants and a sleep shirt. She'd insisted since they were at the O'Malley's house. Normally she liked just nighties and panties.

"If you're dressed, then I'm dressed. Them's the rules." He didn't want her to see his bandage. It would upset her. She'd try to hide it, but he could always tell.

"Drake that's a stupid-assed rule. Strip."

He pulled back the covers, and slipped in beside her. "We're just taking a quick nap." Even through their layers of clothing, he could feel her softness, her warmth.

"Ahhh." She made a strangled sound.

"What is it, Baby?"

"Nothing."

He stroked back her hair, and tilted her chin up so he could look at her. She was biting her lip, a sure sign that she was holding something in.

"Tell me, Honey."

"I missed this. I try not to be so needy, but no matter what, in the middle of the night, I ache with the need to be in your arms."

He pulled her closer, tangling their legs together, but still conscious of her bruise. "God, Karen." He didn't know what to say.

"See, I shouldn't have told you. Now you're going to feel guilty about leaving me. And you can't. During the days I can cope. It's the nights that are the problem. I need to get over this."

Drake thought about the moonlit depths of the jungle and how his soul reached for Karen's. He understood. "I hate that you felt lonely, but I'm glad we're in this together."

Her head jerked, and she stared at him. "Drake?"

"I thought you knew," he whispered. "In the darkest hours of the night, I long for your embrace."

How could she have been so stupid? So naïve?

Maybe it was now that she was a mother of a baby boy that she could finally see the vulnerability in Drake's midnight eyes. He really did need her as much as she needed him. She'd never once doubted that he'd loved her. She'd known that, like she knew the sun rose in the East, but need?

"Karen, maybe somehow I would survive without you, but it would be as half a man."

She plastered her front against him, hugging him as close as he would allow. "Hold me tighter."

He kissed the top of her head, nuzzling her hair. She always used the honeysuckle shampoo because she knew he liked the smell. She kissed his throat, and he groaned. Now she had him. He clasped the back of her neck and rubbed. That meant he was hungry for a kiss.

His mouth slammed onto hers. A claiming. His tongue thrust into her mouth, and she sucked him in, needing his taste, needing everything he had to give. But even as she welcomed him, she felt his ferocious need, it was more than hunger or lust. It was as if she was as necessary to him as water or air.

One hand moved along her back, pushing her closer to his chest, but even in the heat of passion he was careful of her abdomen. Her Drake, a caretaker to the end. She felt the ridge of his erection and shoved herself against him. She desperately needed to make love to this man who meant everything to her.

He slowly broke off their kiss. "Slow down, Honey."

"Please don't say that. Please."

"I didn't lock the door. Anyone could walk in." His tone was regretful. Karen took in great big gulps of air.

"Go lock the door."

"Do you really mean that?" His expression said he knew the truth.

"Dammit, I'm such a kindergarten teacher." She beat her head against his chest.

"Hey, don't make fun of my hot teacher. She's the woman I fell in love with. We'll be really quiet tonight under the covers."

"Do you promise?" It sounded like such a long time away.

"I promise. In the meantime, I want to hold you while we sleep. Is that okay?"

"God, yes." She tangled her hands in his hair that had grown longer while he'd been gone. "But can I have one more kiss. Just a soft one? To tide me over."

He gave her a wicked grin.

HOURS LATER, Karen set her laptop aside and grinned at Angie Donatelli. "How'd you get stuck playing nursemaid?"

Angie grinned as she held Andrew. "I have a gun and I'm not afraid to use it."

"What?" Karen was sure she had misheard.

"Just kidding, I called first dibs. All the other girls were pissed, let me tell you." Angie had the same drawl as Jack, despite her name she was born and raised in Texas. "But it is true, I do have a gun, which I have been known to use from time to time."

"You have?" Karen was fascinated.

"Part of the job."

"Oh yeah, Drake told me, you were a private investigator back in Texas."

"Yep, took over my granddaddy's operation."

"What are you going to do now that you've moved to San Diego?" Karen eyed Angie warily. She wasn't as confident holding Andrew as the other women had been. Of course, everybody had to learn sometime, didn't they? "Do you want to sit down in the chair?"

"No, I'm fine," Angie said as she walked another circuit around the bedroom. "I'm thinking about getting into cyber-security. Not for me, more for Finn." She shifted Andrew, so he was cradled in her arms instead of on her shoulder. God love her boy, he was smiling contentedly. He was definitely Drake's son, he could handle any situation. "Is there anything I can help with?" Angie asked, nodding toward the laptop in Karen's lap.

"No, I have it covered."

"What *are* you working on?"

Karen considered what to share with Angie. She knew that Drake considered Finn one of his closest friends. "There are still some last-minute arrangements for the wedding that need to be straightened out."

"Like what?"

"Has anyone ever told you that you're persistent?"

Angie laughed. "All the damn time." She came and sat down on the bed beside Karen. "Do you know my story?"

Karen shook her head.

"We're both hooked up with two of the hardest heads in Midnight Delta. You know about Finn, right? His struggles?"

This time Karen nodded.

"He hated needing help, it hurt to watch him. It was at the point that if he didn't bend he was going to break."

Karen got where she was going. "I'm not going to break."

"Sweetie, is there anything I can do to help you?" Angie asked gently. "If not help you, how about venting, wouldn't it be nice to just tell someone what's got you tied up in knots?"

Was she that obvious?

"It's really not that big of a deal," Karen protested one last time, but it wasn't as heartfelt.

"If the way your biting your lip is any indication, it is."

Karen blew her hair off her forehead. "The band we booked, broke up. So now I need to find a DJ on short notice. I've been sending out SOS e-mails and making calls."

"Damn, I'm sorry. Is that it?" Angie asked perceptively.

"How'd you guess?"

"I'm a private investigator. You end up with good instincts."

Karen pushed away her laptop, and held out her hands for her son. Angie gently handed him over.

"Will you let me help?" Angie persisted.

Karen caressed Andrew's head and then looked up into Angie's warm eyes.

"I don't think you can. I've tried every angle. I don't think there's going to be any food, except for Sophia's desserts for the wedding. And we'll just have to make do with a karaoke machine." All hope of the wedding she had wanted was fading away. She had wanted Drake to have a memory he would cherish.

Andrew started to cry. He always started to cry when she got upset, it was almost like he had Mommy radar. It was just one more way she was failing.

"Karen, you're just too close to this, you can't see the forest for the trees."

"What forest? What trees?" Drake asked.

Shit, she hadn't heard him come in over Andrew's cries.

"Never mind," she told Drake.

"Angie, spill it," Drake demanded.

"It's nothing. We're just having a little girl talk."

Drake walked over and picked up Andrew. He rubbed

circles on his tummy and that settled him. "Ladies, you need to come clean, or I'm just going to grab my soon-to-be-wife's laptop when she's sleeping."

"You don't know my password." Karen huffed.

"You changed it to Andrew's birthday, only backwards. Seriously, you need to come up with a better one."

"How did you know that?"

"Baby, you told it to me two days ago when you wanted me to order more diapers, don't you remember?"

"Oh." She had told him, but she'd forgotten. What was wrong with her?

He kissed the top of her head. "Now tell me what's up and I'll take care of it. The apartment is cleaned out. Mr. Albertson has done his inspection. We get our full deposit back."

"What about that grape juice stain on the carpet?" she asked.

"I don't know what to tell you, he overlooked it and gave us the full refund."

"Just how many of you guys were standing there when he did his walk-thru?" Angie asked.

"Just three of us," Drake said innocently.

"So, three Navy SEALs against poor Mr. Albertson. Something tells me we could have gotten away with the carpet being torn out and we would have gotten our deposit back. That is so not cool." Karen stared at him.

"It wasn't cool that he knew I was out of town, you had a newborn and he got you to agree to leave in less than a week. He's lucky I didn't have a man to man conversation with his ass."

Karen sighed.

"He has a point," Angie said.

"Now tell me what's got you upset, Honey."

"Nothing."

"Don't lie to me. You're upset. Now that the apartment is cleaned out, I can focus on the next thing. Is it the wedding? Tell me what it is, and I'll take care of it." He pulled up Andrew's shirt and blew a soft raspberry on his stomach. God, he was adorable with their son. Drake looked up at her from under his eyelashes. "Karen?"

"Fine. The caterer went out of business, and the band broke up. We don't have food, and we don't have music."

"We still have a preacher?"

"Yes."

"Have your dress?"

"Yes."

"Everybody RSVP?"

"Yes."

"Still have the venue on Catalina?"

"Yes."

"Then this is workable."

Karen ground her teeth. He made everything sound like a damned SEAL operation. That was when she saw it. He was favoring his right arm. How had she missed that before?

"Drake, were you injured?"

He flushed and didn't answer.

"Drake Jefferson Avery, you answer me this instant."

"It's just a scratch."

"Come here." She pointed to a spot beside her on the bed that Angie quickly vacated.

"Seriously, Karen, it's nothing."

He was wearing a flannel shirt over a T-Shirt. "Give me Andrew, and show me your arm." He handed her the baby, then took off the over shirt. She saw the butterfly bandages.

"It's a bullet wound, isn't it?"

"It barely grazed me." She had to swallow back nausea.

"Karen, Honey, just breathe. It was nothing, the guys had my back." She nodded. Out of the corner of her eye she saw Angie leave Evie and Aiden's guest room.

Sitting down on the bed, he cupped her cheeks. "It's nothing. You hear me? It's nothing."

She breathed through her mouth. Nothing. She had to get that through her head. This is what he did. This was the man she was going to marry. The man she loved with all of her heart. This is what she'd signed up for.

It was then she saw it. Drake was seriously worried. Andrew in one arm, she cupped his cheek with her other hand. "I'm good," she promised. He let out a breath, and kissed the tip of her nose.

"Good, because we have a wedding to plan."

Oh shit. She didn't like the sound of that.

9

"I LOOKED AT YOUR YELP REVIEWS, I WAS REALLY IMPRESSED by the lobster ravioli. One customer called it sublime." Drake tapped his pen against the list he had printed out.

"Oh, you no longer serve that? What about the spinach ravioli?" God, he had to find some damn thing to compliment her on. Something. Anything.

"Which YELP review was I looking at?" Damn. He typed YELP into his browser. It wasn't loading. "It was the one by Anonymous. I'm looking at it right now, they also said that your lasagna was the best they ever had," he lied.

Drake listened and frowned. "Look Lady, I don't know how he could have eaten so many different dishes in one sitting either. Maybe he's reporting for his whole party. You're the owner, right? Aren't you happy you got a good review?" He listened to her answer.

"Good." He smiled. At last, something positive.

"The reason I was calling is to see if you could do something a little out of the ordinary." Drake played up his Southern accent. He knew a lot of women loved that.

"Well, you see, I wanted to order enough food for two

hundred people. It's really only one hundred people, but there are a lot of big men, so we need double portions."

He listened.

"Yes ma'am, I know you don't cater. But think of it as a large take-out order. I saw on your website that you do take-out orders."

Drake pulled the phone away from his ear.

"Ma'am, I'm not trying to pull a fast one. It's not like I'm asking you to deliver the food, but that would be awfully nice if you would." He put a smile in his voice.

He had to turn down the volume on his phone or his ear was going to start bleeding.

"Ma'am, we haven't even talked about prices, I would pay more than your normal rates."

He listened with the phone away from his head.

"It's on the second Saturday of December." He listened to her some more. "No, I'm not trying to shut down your restaurant for a day."

He sighed as her voice rose another octave.

"No, I didn't know that was one of your biggest nights of the year. How in the hell could I have known that?" Drake asked irritably. He crossed Mama's Catalina Ristorante off his list of potential caterers.

"I really want to thank you for your time," he said nicely.

He hung up. "Shrew." He sighed. It had taken time to be able to track down the owners of those six restaurants in Catalina. They hadn't all ended up screaming. Why the hell had she taken his request as a personal offense? Drake hit his forehead against Aiden's desk.

"Careful with the furniture."

Fuck.

"You just had to come in on stealth mode and see that. Not cool, O'Malley." Drake glowered at his brother-in-law.

"Not my fault you were talking so loud you couldn't hear my coming down the hall."

"I didn't wake Karen, did I?"

"The door was open, I peeked in, she and Andrew are still asleep."

Drake settled back in the chair, relieved that she hadn't heard his failed efforts.

"What the hell is going on, anyway?"

"I'm arranging for caterers for the wedding. Then I need to rustle up a DJ, actually I'd prefer a band."

"Cutting it a little close, aren't you?" Aiden asked as he sat down across from him in the leather chair and put his foot over his knee.

Drake got up, crossed the room and shut the door. Aiden chuckled. "Pussy whipped much?"

"Give it a rest," Drake growled. "My sister has you on the shortest leash imaginable."

Aiden gave a satisfied smile.

"Wipe that grin off your face. That's my sister you're smiling about." Drake reminded him as he sat down behind the desk. "Mr. Rich Guy, do you know any caterers on Catalina Island?"

"Nope, but if you throw money at a situation, you can get what you need."

"Goddammit, don't you think I've tried that?" Drake burst out. "The last broad I just called yelled at me, said I was trying to ruin her business."

"You're not thinking out of the box."

Drake just stared at Aiden. "Are you suggesting I start calling private citizens of Catalina and see if they want to cook for my wedding?"

"Again, my friend, you are not thinking big enough. Sophia is getting you her desserts from San Clemente, right?

She's bringing them over on the boat."

Oh for the love of God, Aiden was absolutely right. He'd been going about this all wrong. "Get out of here," he commanded.

"This is my house. My office," Aiden said without heat.

"Yeah, but you knew what you were getting into when you invited us to stay. Get the hell out."

Aiden chuckled and eased out of the chair and headed for the door. "Let me know if you need any help."

"I've got this."

"Never doubted it."

———

DRAKE so badly wanted to carry Karen up the stairs to their new home. Instead he followed a half step behind her so that if she had any problems he would be there to catch her.

"Stop it," she hissed. "I'm perfectly fine."

"Of course, you are."

"It's been a week since I left the hospital."

"This time."

She stuck out her tongue.

He laughed.

"Seriously, Drake I had my check-up three days ago. Go take Andrew from Piper and leave me alone." She stepped onto the porch and seemed fine. He turned and double-timed it down the stairs to help Piper extract Andrew from the car seat.

"You better stop it," his sister advised.

"What?" he asked innocently. "I'm just caring for my wife."

"Fiancée. And you better remember that. At the rate you're going, she might not agree to be your wife."

"Tinkerbell, bite your tongue," he growled as he lifted Andrew out of the back of the car.

"I'm serious big brother, you need to back off."

"You can't be serious, you had to call an ambulance, she was in the hospital when I got home. I almost lost her in the delivery room. She needs as much TLC as she can possibly get. No stress for Karen, got it?"

Piper wilted under his harsh words.

Damn.

He put Andrew up on his shoulder, and then wrapped his other arm around his small, youngest sister. "I'm sorry, I didn't mean to come off so strong. I'm just a little freaked out about Karen's health."

"S'okay." She shrugged out of his hold.

"Piper, won't you listen to me?"

She headed towards the stairs. "I've listened enough," she called over her shoulder and ran up the stairs. By the time Drake made it inside he couldn't find either Karen or Piper in the living room or kitchen. He called out and only Karen answered.

"I'm in the nursery," she said. He grinned, thinking how pleased she'd be. He walked down the hall and found her standing in the middle of the room with her fists clenched.

"What did you do?"

"What do you mean?" he asked.

"What did you do?" she asked again.

"I surprised you?" he asked cautiously.

"There's a mural with an ocean with orca whales, then there are evergreens and a bear in the woods. Are those salmon?" It covered one whole wall, the other three walls were blue with fish decals artfully placed on them.

"A friend of a friend of Sophia's painted it. I wanted it to look like Alaska. Isn't it great?" He'd worked damned hard thinking of something that might please her. It wasn't anything that he would have chosen, but hell, it was her home state. The mural might be a little over the top. There was the octopus hugging a sea otter that was a little disconcerting.

"Why'd you think I want a nursery with grizzly bears on the walls?"

"We never talked about it, so I didn't know, but I thought you might like something that made you think of home?" his voice went up on the last word.

He watched as she shut her eyes and breathed deeply. This was not going like he'd expected. He eyed the bassinette, and put a sleeping Andrew down before Karen and he had their little 'talk'.

"Didn't you see the orange and white striped curtains?" She asked through gritted teeth.

"The kitchen curtains?"

"No, the Tennessee Volunteer curtains."

He saw the green fire shooting from her eyes.

"Honey, what are you talking about?"

"Have I ever once said anything about wanting our son to grow up underwater? Did I say that I had been on the Enchantment Under the Sea prom decorating committee and it was the highlight of my life? Did I say I missed Alaska and I wanted to move back?"

"Well no," he answered carefully.

"Then why on God's green Earth did you think I would want this?"

"I didn't know what you wanted for the nursery, and this seemed like something you might like, and it was blue."

He watched her take a deep breath and paste a false smile on her face that didn't reach her eyes. "Why didn't you ask me?"

"You've been sick. You had to take care of everything on your own, I wanted to handle this for you." He paused and thought about her question.

"Drake, don't you think this is something we should have discussed? Don't you think I would have wanted to be involved in decorating my son's nursery?"

Oh shit, she was right. He walked over to her and tried to put his arms around her. She rebuffed him. It reminded him of what Piper had just done. "You're totally right, I should have talked to you about this."

She nodded. "Yes," she said tightly, "you should have." Then she let out a deep breath. "But I'm to blame too."

He perked up. "Yeah?"

"I did basically the same thing. I didn't discuss what I was doing with you. I was doing something that I thought you would like. I wanted to surprise you."

He smirked.

"Before you get all high and mighty Drake Jefferson, there's one huge difference."

"What?"

"I *like* what I chose for you. Do you *like* the octopus wrestling thing you have going on?"

Drake choked back a laugh and shook his head. "No, can't say that I do. What were you going to surprise me with?"

"Didn't you just hear me say the white and orange curtains were for the Tennessee Volunteers?"

"You'd do that for me? You'd decorate his room after my favorite college football team?"

"Honey, the Tennessee Volunteers are *our* favorite team, bar none. Didn't we get the premium cable package just so we could watch them? Have we ever missed a game? I bet I can name the entire defensive line right this very second, you wanna listen?"

God, she was hot when she talked football.

"We both fucked up?"

"Don't swear in front of Andrew." She scowled.

"One, he's sleeping. Two, he can't cogitate. Three, he's going to be a SEAL so he needs to know these words."

Karen rolled her eyes.

"I better call Mason and Billy over to help paint the walls orange."

"Are you out of your mind? We're painting the walls white, and putting orange accents around the room. Orange walls would look terrible." She shuddered. "I have an orange and white baby lamp, and a little matching orange football blanket for the crib."

"There's a Vols blanket? That is so cool. Where'd you get that?"

"I got it all on-line, except for the pillows, those Maddie sent to me."

"You are not painting a damn thing. You are still on lock-down young lady." He kissed the tip of her nose. "Billy and Mason would love to help."

"Fine, go and round up Billy and Mason. I need to find out why Piper stormed into her room."

"I'll just call Mason to buy the paint and he and Billy can come on over," he said as he went over to the bassinette to check on Andrew.

She walked up beside him. They both took a moment to stare at their son.

"You know, looking at him, makes everything else seem like a minor problem. He's the most important thing in the world," she whispered.

"Both of you are."

"Our family is. You're just as important to me, as I am to you."

He pulled her close. "I know Sweetheart. You didn't watch near as much football until you met me. Don't think I don't know what you do for me."

"Hey, I love it now," she protested.

He kissed her temple. "Thanks for coming into my life Karen."

"I wouldn't have missed a moment of this, now go over to Mason's house and ask him nicely to help," she said softly. Then she lifted her head in panic. "Wait, I don't want to hurt Sophia's artist friend's feelings."

"It'll be our little secret. Mason and Billy will take it to their grave."

"Good. So, get going."

"I'm staying here."

"No, you're not, you're going over to Mason's," she said as she pulled him away from the bassinette, so they wouldn't disturb Andrew.

"I'm not leaving," he said firmly.

"Yes. Yes, you are."

"You're going to end up doing something stupid like trying to unpack boxes when you shouldn't."

She hitched in a deep breath, and stared at Drake incredulously.

"I didn't mean it like that," he tried to hug her, but she backed up a step.

"Drake, we have to talk this out. It can't go on like this." Her voice was low and sad.

He knew he'd fucked up, but she sounded so serious, it scared the piss out of him.

"You see me differently than the woman you first met. I'm now one more person in your life you have to take care of."

"Yes, you are. You and Andrew are the most important people in my world. I would fight to the death to take care of you." Once again, he reached out to her, and once again she backed away.

"Hear me out, okay?" Her voice was tremulous. God, what was wrong?

"Sure Honey, I'll listen. Say what you have to say." Why wouldn't she let him hold her?

"This isn't me. You know?"

He shook his head. He had no idea what she was talking about.

She stood there and cocked her head to the side. He could see her thinking. "Give me a second, okay? I want to say this right."

"Take all the time you need." If it was going to be bad, then he could wait a hundred years to hear it.

"Oh dammit, now I've made you anxious." She stepped forward and wrapped her arms around his waist. Well this was good. This was really good. She tilted her head back and looked at him. "How many people have you had to take care of in your life?" she asked softly.

"I don't know."

"Of course, you don't, because there have been so many your soul can't keep count, let alone your head."

Where was she going with this?

"How many people have taken care of you?"

"Mason. My team. You."

She jerked away from him, her eyes round.

"Me? You know I've wanted to take care of you?"

"Honey, there is no *want* in that sentence. You have taken care of me. You shelter me. You have right from the start."

She continued to stare at him in disbelief.

"You didn't think I knew that? Karen, I've never felt so loved, so cared for, in my entire life."

Her eyes filled with tears. "Hey, don't cry. Baby, don't cry. What's wrong?"

"But I'm not sheltering you anymore. I'm an anchor. I'm just one more person you have to take care of," she hiccupped.

He stared at her in disbelief. He swiped at her tears with his thumbs. "Jesus, is that why you're acting like a crazy woman and trying to do everything?"

Her eyes glinted. It could go either way, she could hit him for calling her a crazy woman, or she might fess up. Finally, she nodded. He crouched lower so he could wrap his arms around her waist and lift her up so they were face to face.

"This is a partnership you goof. If I came back wounded and you had to take care of me for a year, would you think less of me? Would you consider me an anchor?"

"Of course not," she vehemently denied. "How could you even ask that?"

He just stared at her. And stared at her. And stared at her.

She blew the bangs up off her forehead. "I might have had a flaw in my thinking."

"You might could have," he agreed solemnly.

She rested her hands on his shoulders. "Uhmm, you know you might have added to this problem a wee bit yourself big guy."

Damn. He was so hoping to get off Scott free. "I'm listening."

"Maybe you should put me down."

"I'm more than capable of holding onto my woman,

especially for the important conversations. Say what you have to say."

"Okay, you've been acting like a crazy man. Care to share why?"

"Can you be more specific than 'Crazy Man'?"

"Since you've been home this time, you've gone into hyperdrive. I feel like you don't think I'm capable of putting one step in front of the other without your help."

"I should never have left. Not after having almost lost you. Not with Andrew so young. I should never have left."

"Of course, you should have. Honey, I was the one who told you to go."

He didn't hear her. He thought about that moment when Piper had called him damn near a year ago. His little sister had been afraid for her life. Their dad was intent on killing her. Drake had left her, and the rest of his sisters, to that kind of horror. Just like he'd abandoned Karen nineteen days ago.

"Drake! You're not listening to me."

"What?"

Andrew started crying. "I have to feed Andrew. Come with me into the bedroom." He released his hold on her, then like a balm, she laid a kiss on his chest, right over his heart. "Follow me. I need to understand what you're not telling me."

———

THEIR BEDROOM HAD BEEN SET up perfectly. The dresser was where she would have wanted it placed. The light mint wall color exactly matched the new duvet cover she had purchased. If she had to guess, Piper had a lot of input on this room.

"Do you like it?" Drake asked hopefully.

"I love it," she assured him.

He grinned, then he guided her to the bed where he sat down with his back to the headboard. "Rest against me." He held out his arms, and she turned around and sank back against him. Even with Andrew raging, she felt comfortable.

"You need to calm down, Little Guy," he said, reaching around and putting out his finger so Andrew could latch on with one angry fist. With his other hand, somehow Drake was able to deftly unbutton her top, and then unlatch the cup of her nursing bra. He stroked her full breast, and she felt it throughout her body.

"God, Drake, celibacy sucks."

He chuckled, then kissed her neck. "Tonight, let's see what we can do about creative ways to pleasure you."

"And you. I refuse for this to be a one-way street." She wiggled her ass against his crotch and laughed when he groaned.

"Are we done arguing?" he asked as he cupped the back of Andrew's head and guided him to her nipple.

"We're not arguing, we're discussing. I want to discuss why you think you can't leave me."

He was silent. He kept stroking her breast.

"Drake?"

"Let's talk about this later."

She knew that tone. He didn't use it often, but her man was frustrated, and not sexually. This was the perfect time to talk. This was the safest, most loving place they could ever have together. They could work out world peace right now.

"Tell me Drake. We need to get it out in the open. I can handle it, and you need to get it off your chest."

"Dammit Karen, I don't know which way is up, and I fucking hate it. I'm not like this. I just pick a course of action and go for it." He said low and vehemently so as not to disturb Andrew."

That was the truth. "What are you conflicted about?"

"You were wrong about something and so was I. I could depend on Trenda and Evie. I knew they had my back and the girls backs. They would call for help when something was up. Hell, they've raised Piper in their image."

This time he was louder, and Andrew started to fidget. She stroked his cheek and he went back to suckling.

"What are you saying Drake?"

"You asked why I went into hyperdrive? Because you've been hiding shit from me. You did a one-eighty from the woman I knew. Basically, you lost your damn mind."

So much for being able to handle anything when she was in Drake's arms and nursing Andrew. That hurt. It hurt a lot. Why? Because it was true.

"The Karen I know and love would ask for help. Trenda and Evie did when it got bad. You say that you've got it now. But do you really? Because you scared the piss out of me. And I can't imagine going on a mission again unless I know for sure you're safe and you'll ask for help. You do that, then you're not being a burden, you're being an asset."

"Well then." It was all she could say while she gathered her thoughts.

"What does that mean?"

"I think I just met Mr. SEAL team second in command."

"Uhhhm, maybe."

"So am I supposed to say yes Sir?"

"I'm not an officer. You just say yes. Then if you were Clint you would make a smart-ass comment like your head is now out of your ass."

Karen bit her lip. "How about, I love you?"

"That would be Jack. He has a crush on me."

Karen laughed. Andrew let out a huff as he lost his meal ticket. She brought his head back to her nipple.

"Damn Drake. Do you know how sexy you are when you're smart?"

"You're not mad at me?" he asked tentatively.

"Baby, you hit the nail on the head. How could I be mad? I'm not even really hurt by what you said. I'm relieved. I was going about this all wrong. I was coming to that conclusion on my own, but in your own tactful and loving way, you got me to the answer faster."

"Finn said he missed our special talks," he murmured into her hair.

"I'm sure he did," she said wryly.

"But there's more."

"Oh God, I don't think I can handle more," she said. "For real Drake. More?"

"No, this isn't so bad, I promise. Now that I know that you'll ask for help, I still want to do a little bit more to make sure you're safe."

"Like what? What would make me and Andrew safer?"

"If someone other than just Piper was living with you," he answered immediately.

"Who?"

"Ideally one of my teammates, but they would be on a mission with me." He sighed.

Damn, it sounded like he wanted to hire a personal protection service for her. Yep, her man had lost his ever-loving mind. She needed to go at this from another angle.

"It must be weird being the first one on your team to have a child. What are the others thinking? Are they planning on having kids?"

"Well Dare basically has kids. Of course, they're grown. Sawyer's going to be eighteen any day now. Charlotte is turning fifteen if she isn't already. But Georgie is a special case."

"Is Dare nervous leaving them at home alone with Rylie."

"Of course not. But then Rylie was caring for them for years without Dare being in the picture." Drake explained.

Well that tact wasn't going to work.

"What about some of the others? How about Jack and Beth, are they planning on having kids anytime soon?"

Drake's cheek had been resting against hers, he tilted her head, so they could look at one another. "I wouldn't be surprised if they were pregnant next year. Beth has mother written all over her."

"Well, how is Jack going to cope with Beth being alone with their child while he's alone on missions?"

"He won't. Mark my words, with his money, they'll suddenly have a live-in couple to take care of the house. One as a gardener or some such shit, one to help with the kid. You can be damn sure that the man will have 'skills'."

"He's going to hire a mercenary to live with them?"

"Damn straight."

"That's just crazy."

"Look at it from Jack's point-of-view, his stepdad is as rich as Midas and that money's flowed Jack's way. It's made him a target. He's not going to leave his wife and kid unprotected. I'm just stunned he hasn't made it happen already."

"And Clint and Lydia?" Karen asked. "They're not targets. They're not rich. They're like us."

"God knows when they'll reproduce, but Clint will have the best security system in the world."

"Fine, get us that."

Drake's stroking fingers stalled. His entire body went still. "I could do that," he said slowly.

Andrew was winding down. "He's going to need to be burped," she stalled. Karen pulled their son away, and Drake took him. He grabbed the baby towel off the nightstand and put a conked-out Andrew on his shoulder. Karen arranged her clothing back in place. Before she could sit back up, Drake had her cuddled up against his other shoulder.

"Thank you for listening. I'm sorry I got so pissy."

"I don't know if pissy is the right word," she teased. "I'm thinking commanderish. It was kind of hot."

"You mean like when you get all schoolmarm? I got to tell you, you sure punch my clock."

She scowled at him.

"See. See right there? That look you're giving me. Scorching."

"You're a nut."

"You just admitted you like me being in command," he reminded her.

And she did. Especially in bed.

"So the command decision is that we're installing a high-tech security system," he announced. Then he pulled her close, his eyes glimmering.

"I think that's a workable plan." She smiled before his mouth closed in on hers.

10

Drake felt like a heel. This was the first time he and Tinkerbell had ever been at odds this long. When he had tried to make amends that night, she said she couldn't talk, she had to study. He had really blown it.

"What's wrong?" Karen asked as she looked up from putting Andrew into his sleeper.

"Piper. She's not talking to me." He'd already told Karen what he'd said to his sister.

"Try again tomorrow," Karen suggested as she tickled Andrews tummy. Drake smiled when he saw Andrew's little baby smile. The kid smiled like his mother, with his whole heart.

"Do you think it's going to scar our boy if he sleeps in the Under the Sea nursery tonight?" Drake asked Karen.

"Why? What do you have in mind?"

"I want a little quality time with my wife."

"I'm not your wife," she reminded him.

He came up behind her as she picked up Andrew from the bed. He pushed back her auburn hair and kissed behind her ear. "In my heart, you're already my wife. You were my wife that day I picked you up in the snow." He felt her tremble.

"I suppose Andrew can spend a couple of hours in Alaska. We'll check on him in a while."

Drake scraped his teeth against the chords in her neck. She shivered. He loved how responsive she was. "Give him to me," he whispered.

"I'll get ready for bed," she said as he headed for the door. He went down the hall to the nursery.

"You going to be a good boy for Daddy for a couple of hours?" Drake asked as he put his son in the crib. "I have plans, and I could sure use a solid."

Andrew blinked slowly as he snuggled onto the mattress. Drake couldn't believe the amount of love that swelled up as he looked down at the tiny scrap of humanity in the little blue sleeper. "God kid, you're the shit, you know that?"

Andrew sighed as he drifted off to sleep, totally oblivious to his old man's heartfelt words. Just as well, now Drake needed to focus on Andrew's mama. He placed a kiss on the back of his son's head and turned on the nightlight. He assured himself that Piper's door was tightly shut then headed back towards the master bedroom.

The room was dark. He saw the green dot of the baby monitor, but that was it. He took care of that with the flip of a switch. It still cracked him up that Karen was bashful.

"Drake," she protested, "not the overhead lights."

He looked at her in a beautiful silk nightie that he hadn't seen in months. "You turn on the bedside lamp, and I'll turn off the overhead. Is it a deal?" He leaned against the wall and watched as she stretched across the bed to reach the light. The nightie barely covered her fuller breasts, it was a beautiful sight to behold.

"There," she said with exasperation.

"Now the other one."

She gave him the evil eye, but then scooched over, and reached. God, he was ready to come from just watching her. What was it going to be like when he finally got his hands on her? He knew they couldn't have sex, but Oh Lordy, the fun they were going to have tonight.

"Drake, turn off the light."

He slammed off the light and prowled over to the side of the bed where she was. She grinned up at him. He put one knee on the bed and put his arms on either side of her, effectively caging her in. "I'm going to eat you up," he said.

"Me first." She smiled.

"Nope." He tugged at the thin strap on her green nightie. "As much as I love this, I want it off."

"Uhhm. I was kind of hoping we could start with you."

His head whipped up to look at her face. She wasn't kidding. Her hands were already at his belt. "No, you've waited long enough. I want to take care of you," she said emphatically. She had his belt unbuckled and was working on the button of his jeans when he caught sight of her eyes. She looked panicked. What the hell?

Drake gently clasped her hands in one of his, then rolled them over so that she landed on his chest. He stroked his other hand down her back. Once. Twice. He kept doing it until she settled. "Do you know how much I love you?"

He felt her breath sigh out. "I know."

"I love lying here like this. I dream of this when we're apart."

"So do I, Drake. I dream of you a lot. I wake up hugging your pillow. I never wash your pillowcase after you leave. I need to keep your scent near so I can hold onto you."

He swallowed. He hadn't known that.

He tugged at the strap of her nightie again, and she tensed. "What's wrong?"

"Nothing." She breathed the word quietly into his neck. He didn't believe her for an instant. Slowly he rolled them over so he was looking down at her. She avoided his glance, which was fine, there were plenty of other things to look at. To savor. God, he'd been wanting a chance to touch her for what seemed like forever. His hand hovered over her waist. She yanked it up to her breast.

"Why'd you do that?"

"Uhm."

"Miss Schoolteacher, 'uhmm' is not an answer. Not that I don't appreciate the bounty, but why'd you move my hand? Are you hurting?"

She shook her head, letting her hair cover her face. She'd pulled that trick in the past, he wasn't letting it fly now. He brushed it back, so he could see her pretty green eyes. "Honey, what's bothering you?"

"Nothing," she repeated.

"Well if it's nothing, then I get to do what I want." He pushed up onto his knees and in one smooth move he had her divested of her nightgown.

"Drake!" she let out a soft shriek.

He saw that she was wearing purple panties. God, it was just like the first time they'd ever been intimate. "Purple." He grinned.

She tugged at the covers and he pulled them out of her hands. "Nope, this body is mine for the night. At least until Andrew gets hungry, and even then, I'm not sure he's going to win, because Daddy has been starving for a long time."

"You can't mean that." She had her arms crossed over her belly, and everything became crystal clear in an instant. He wanted to wrench her hands away and tell her she was out of her mind. In fact, he was a hairsbreadth away from doing so, but he looked up into her fragile expression and memories washed over him.

Karen had only had one other experience before being with him. She'd been practically a virgin when she'd first come into his arms, and it was like that again. Despite everything they had gone through, or maybe because of what she *had* gone through, she was delicate, and it was up to him to soothe, woo and then seduce her.

"Drake?"

"Right here, Baby." He stroked the back of his knuckles down her arm until reaching the tips of her fingers, relishing it when she quivered. He laced his fingers with hers, then brought her hand to his mouth and kissed it. Out of the corner of his eye he saw her splay her other hand over the scar on her tummy. Hell, he'd kissed it before. She had to know he wasn't bothered by it, didn't she? That was a badge of honor.

He brought her arm up and looped it around his shoulder, then bent in for a kiss. She responded beautifully. Soon all thought of her response was forgotten, as he lost himself in the wonder of her passion. Sweet and wild. He thrust his tongue into the warm, wet welcome of her mouth and he groaned when he felt the fingers of her other hand dig into his hair, her nails scraping his scalp.

Karen bit his lip, and his cock throbbed in response. Then she had the gall to laugh. She knew what she'd done. He reared back and looked into her shining green eyes. There was his girl. He felt moisture against his chest, then the sparkle left her eyes, and horror replaced it.

"What? Karen, what?"

She closed her eyes and shook her head. Drake looked down at his chest and saw a little bit of wet. Then he laughed. She opened one eye and stared up at him. He snagged one of the baby towels off the nightstand. "We might need this. One of the guys said you leaking during sex meant I was doing it right."

"What?!" She hit him on his shoulder. "You talked about our sex life?"

"Not our sex life. He was talking about post-pregnancy sex. He explained a few things and I listened. Now weren't you biting my lip? I liked that part." Drake pressed his lips to Karen's. She turned her head.

"This doesn't bother you?"

He looked at her in amazement, then grabbed her hand and dragged it to the front of his jeans. She cupped his erection and he groaned again. "Jesus, Karen, hell yes I'm bothered. You and your body bother me a lot." He could tell it was time for the blunt talk portion of their conversation.

He sat up and then she let out a squeak when he easily lifted her into his lap. She was laid out like a bounty where she couldn't hide a damn thing.

"Honey, you seem to be under the misapprehension that this tiny little scar upsets me. Have I missed something. Do my scars turn you off?"

She gave a slight shake of her head.

"Really?"

"Of course not."

"Then how could I be turned off by this tiny little thing that you earned by bringing our son into the world?"

"Tiny?"

"Yes, tiny. Compared to mine, this is absolutely delicate. Just like you are. Well except for your luscious breasts. My God woman, just watching you walk around the house about gives me a heart attack. And let's face it, you and I both know why they're bigger, and a little bit of milk between friends isn't a big deal."

"You are too much."

"Bullshit, you always told me I was just right." Drake waggled his eyebrows, and watched in delight as she laughed.

She relaxed in his arms and he took advantage. His hand wandered, and stroked down her side, to her waist, then rested on her hip. She squirmed, and he took that as a good sign. God knew he was squirming. Her hand drifted upwards, spearing through the hair on his chest. Game over.

He had her flat on her back in an instant, her pretty purple panties thrown across the room. She giggled. He would have grinned, but he was too intent on his goal. He was enraptured by her slick pink folds. He parted her flesh and saw his goal. He circled the engorged nub with his finger and she bucked up against him.

"It's too much."

"It's not enough," he disagreed. "It's not nearly enough." He shifted downwards, and nudged her legs further apart so he could settle between them. He touched her with his tongue, savoring her every sigh, her every moan. He could feel her excitement rise higher as she pushed against him. Gently he held her down, forcing her to take more.

"Oh God," she panted.

He smiled and redoubled his efforts, loving the flood of honey that slid over his tongue. She bucked against his hands, and he saw her hands fling outward and grab his pillow. As she bit into it, he ever so gently bit her clit and rasped it back and forth with his tongue. He heard her muffled scream of fulfillment. She slumped back into the mattress and he kissed his way up her body, wrenching the pillow out of her hands and flinging it to the floor, probably next to her purple panties. He grinned down at her.

"Proud of yourself?" she asked.

"Yep."

"Take off those goddamn jeans."

"Your wish is my command." He stood and shucked off his remaining clothes. Her breasts jiggled as she slid off the bed and got down on her knees. He damn near ended up on his at the sight of her. Had he ever been this excited?

She stroked the length of him, then she staggered him even more as she rubbed her cheek against his engorged flesh and breathed him in. "So good," she moaned. "I've missed you."

Her dainty tongue began painting patterns up and down his body, making him shudder, making him need, right before she engulfed him in hot depths of her mouth. He groaned. Karen started a rhythm that felt sublime. It was more than just passion, she made him feel loved. He feathered his fingers through the silk of her hair, and her eyes drifted up to look at him, they were dark green with a fire he had craved for months.

"You're beautiful. You're perfect," he rasped out.

She swirled her tongue against the sensitive underside of his cock and his knees trembled.

"Honey, I'm going to come," he warned.

She let go of his erect flesh with her hand and sucked harder, deeper, and then grasped the back of his thigh, pulling him closer. He was losing his mind, but her meaning was clear.

He shouldn't. But her nails dug into him. His heart and mind filled with the knowledge that he had never been so loved as he shot into space.

11

It was the final fitting of her dress. Damn, they were going to have to take it in a bit. She really had overdone it and worked herself into a frazzle.

"You look beautiful." Piper sighed.

She heard a muffled sound and looked up. Her mom had a Kleenex shoved against her mouth.

"Ahh, Mom."

"You look exquisite. I'd hug you, but I'd get the dress wet."

"Hold on, let me just get two more pins in, then I'll get you out of this, and the hugging can commence." The seamstress smiled. Karen was so happy she had chosen this bridal shop, everyone was so nice.

"My brother is going to lose his shit." Evie grinned.

"I like you." Wilma Eastman wrapped her arm around Evie's waist. "Karen did good choosing Drake, and I inherited six more daughters." Karen watched the look that Evie and Piper shared. Her mom was good for the Avery sisters after the hell their biological mother had put them through. Evie leaned in just a tad. Not too much, because that wouldn't be Evie. But just a little. Yep, her mom rocked.

"Do any of you need to try on your bridesmaid dresses while you're here?" the seamstress asked.

"Nope," Evie said. "Everything is covered."

"Except for our shoes." Piper sighed.

"What are you talking about?" Karen and Wilma asked simultaneously.

"Drake," Piper said. "I mentioned that the color didn't exactly match the dresses, and that we'd decided to go with black patent leather to match the burgundy dresses. Mister Control Freak arranged for shoes to be dyed up in Los Angeles. God knows if they'll get here in time."

"Please say you bought the black shoes," Karen begged.

"Of course," Evie assured her.

"He was all proud of himself that he found a DJ, but then he got so picky about the songs, that the DJ quit. Then he had to find a back-up for the back-up. At the rate we're going, we'll be stuck with a Karaoke machine."

Wilma giggled.

"It's not funny, Mom."

"Yes, it is."

"He's gone full SEAL," Evie said.

"Aiden wouldn't have done this," Karen said.

Evie smirked. "You're right, he wouldn't have. My brother is special," she said using air quotes around the word special. Wilma giggled again.

"Mom, quit laughing."

"I can't help it." Even the seamstress was biting her lip. She sighed. Something needed to be done.

"This is my fault. I made a promise to ask for help if I needed it, so I told him about the caterers and the band falling through. He immediately went into Mr. Fix-It mode."

"Well that explains it."

"He called to ask if there were any flowers that your dad and your brothers were allergic to. Apparently, he didn't want them sneezing during the ceremony. Leif wanted me to ask you if you knew you were marrying someone with obsessive compulsive tendencies." Now her mother was wiping her eyes for a totally different reason.

"God grant me patience," Karen said with a deep sigh.

"An intervention is in order," Piper said.

"To hell with that. Tequila is in order," Evie said.

"I can't," Karen wailed. "I'm breastfeeding."

"Honey, it's not that bad," Wilma said, trying to keep a straight face.

Karen glared at her mother. "Don't even. You don't mean it."

Her mother dissolved into giggles. "You're right, I don't. This is fucking funny."

"Oh God, you're throwing down the F-Bomb."

Evie leaned into Wilma. "I'm adopting your Mom."

"You can have her. She's a traitor."

"I am not. I love my new son-in-law. He's just a bit over-the-top."

"We need an intervention," Piper said again. "And tequila."

"You're not old enough to drink," Karen reminded the young woman.

"Fine, you and I will have milkshakes, while the rest of my sister's drink alcohol and we'll all plan the best way to tell big brother that he needs to pull his head out of his ass."

Karen looked at Piper and realized that she was a little more vehement than normal. This was just Drake being Drake. But even after ten days, there was still something off between the two of them. She needed to have a talk with her before this *intervention* took place.

"So, it's decided. When we pick up the Avery Avalanche tomorrow, we plan. After all, we don't want him telling the preacher how to hold the bible," Evie said.

Karen winced, and Wilma laughed...again.

HER MOM WAS HOLDING court with the Avery girls in the living room. Drake was over at Clint's house figuring out how to build a moat around their townhome. She'd watched Piper go off down the hall to check on Andrew and she followed.

"Everything okay?"

"Nothing fourteen baby wipes couldn't take care of." Piper grinned.

Karen went to the baby dresser and pulled out a new sleeper for her son. "He's powerful," she commiserated.

"Yep. Are you sure you're not feeding him broccoli and asparagus?" Piper asked.

"Hell, I don't even eat that stuff myself." Karen laughed. "I'm a peas and carrots kind of gal."

"Drake must be slipping him some of his wheat grass protein shake."

"Speaking of Drake, he's really upset about the rift between the two of you."

Piper's head shot up. "He's talked to you about it?"

"Of course."

"I'm surprised."

"He feels terrible. He didn't mean to be mean."

Piper stared at her, confusion obvious on her face. "What are you talking about?" she finally asked.

"He said he was short with you the day we moved into the townhome."

"Yeah, he's mad at me. I understand. *I'm* mad at me. I let everyone down."

Karen handed her the yellow sleeper with giraffes on it, and considered her words. There was a lot more to this than Drake thought. "Honey, what are you talking about?"

"I should never have spent the weekend at my friend's house. I should have been here for you. I should have taken better care of you and Andrew." Tears swam in Piper's dark eyes as she picked up her nephew.

"Give him to me." Karen swiftly put her son into his crib and pulled Piper into her arms. "You did nothing wrong."

Piper burst into tears. Karen was dumbfounded. "Piper, Honey, in no way shape or form is anyone holding you to blame for my stupidity."

Piper just shook harder.

Karen tried to get her to look up at her, but she just kept her chin down. "Piper, please look at me." The girl shook her head. "Please, Honey."

"Drake hates me, I know it."

Now it all made sense. "You need to talk to him. He thinks *you're* mad at *him*."

She continued to shake her head.

"Yes, it's true. Listen to me."

"I let him down. You ended up in the hospital. What would have happened if I hadn't come home?"

Karen didn't want to think about it. She'd been an idiot and it was on her. She felt terrible that Piper had shouldered this on herself. She heard the light knock on the door. She looked up and saw Trenda standing in the doorway. She cocked her eyebrow in question. Karen motioned her inside.

"Trenda, stay with Piper, I'm getting my phone. I'm calling Drake home."

"Don't do that," Piper begged.

Andrew whimpered.

Karen loved the fact that Trenda didn't ask any questions, she just put her arms around her little sister. "Let's just let Karen do what she thinks is best."

"But—"

"Trust me Piper. This is all a big misunderstanding. In no way does Drake hold you responsible for a damn thing. He's grateful that you were there to take care of me and Andrew."

Hope shone in Piper's eyes. Karen picked up Andrew and met Trenda's eyes. "I'm going to call Drake. You two wait here. Okay? He's just across the complex."

Karen hustled down the hall to the master bedroom. She could still hear the laughter from the living room. Evie had the margaritas flowing. Aiden would be coming to pick up the girls around midnight. She grabbed her cell phone off the nightstand and called Drake.

"Hi, Honey. How's everything going? Are you having fun?"

"Can you come home?"

"Why? What's wrong? Is Evie misbehaving?"

"Piper's having a meltdown. She's positive that you're mad at her. She believes that she let you down by not taking better care of me when you were away. Jeez, it's like an Avery trait."

"What?"

"She's crying so hard, I can't stand it. Can you come?"

"I'm already out the door."

Karen let out a sigh of relief.

"THERE HE IS. Just the man we were looking for," Zoe said as she blocked his way into the living room with an evil gleam in her eye.

"Not now. Where's Piper?"

God love her, Zoe immediately caught on and backed off.

"Is something wrong?" Maddie asked.

He looked around the room and didn't see Piper, Trenda or Karen. "I think she might be in the nursery," Wilma said.

He gave a curt nod and headed down the hallway. Karen met him at the door, she put her arms around him. "It's going to be okay, Love."

"How could she think I'm mad at her?"

"She won't for much longer, that's the important thing." He took the kiss that she offered then went into the nursery.

"Tinkerbell?" Her wet eyes killed him. She didn't answer. Trenda guided Piper towards him, and then left the room.

"I'm not mad," he said baldly.

"You have to be." Her tone was anguished. "You told me to take care of them right before you left." Had he? He didn't remember. Hell, he might have. He'd told everyone the same thing.

He cupped the back of her head, and pulled her to his chest. She grabbed the front of his T-Shirt and buried her face in it. He felt her hot breath as she tried to get her breathing under control. "Not only am I not mad, I'm fucking grateful to you."

He felt her still. Finally. "You are?" she asked in a high voice.

"Absolutely. Your quick thinking helped save the day."

She stayed silent, so he continued. "You kept your head

and got an ambulance, you stayed with Andrew and made sure he got well. I couldn't have asked for a better person watching over Karen and Andrew."

She looked up at him, a tremulous smile on her face. "I never want to let you down."

"Ah Honey, we're all going to let one another down from time to time, but it's the way we recover that matters."

She hugged him tightly and it felt wonderful.

"Do you know how important you are to me? You and Karen and Andrew?"

"Ahhh, Tink. You were my first baby. I absolutely adore you."

She beamed.

"Shall we go out and join the others?" he asked.

Piper giggled. Drake looked down at her. Not that he didn't like the fact that she was giggling after such a breakdown, but he could tell something was up.

"Piper, you better spill it."

"I don't know what you're talking about. Let's go out to the living room. You can have a margarita or a milkshake." She smiled mischievously.

"I choose beer."

She grabbed his hand and practically dragged him down the hallway. When he reached the living room he tried to catch Karen's eye, but she avoided looking at him by concentrating on her drink. Despite the fact that something was obviously up, seeing Karen sucking on a straw had a marked effect on his body. That was the moment she chose to look up and wink at him. Minx.

"Drake, there's room on the couch between us," Zoe said. She patted a spot between her and her twin Chloe. Well that was good news, he could always depend on Chloe to be a good sport. Zoe and Evie both were evil.

"Hey Chloe," he said as he sat down next to his newly married little sister. "Howya doing?"

"Not good. The shoes you got me turned my feet red," she snarled at him. She lifted up the hem of her jeans and kicked off her ballet flat. Sure enough, her foot was red. "I only wore the damn things for a half hour while I had my dress fitting. Trenda says I have to soak my foot in vinegar and lemon juice, I'm sure Zarek is going to love sleeping with that."

The bad news was, Chloe was well and truly pissed. The good news was, she was well and truly out of her depression. He let out a big laugh, absolutely thrilled about the good news.

"Dammit Drake, this is nothing to laugh about."

"It's just so fucking great that you're raking me over the coals, Sissy. I totally deserve it."

"Yeah, she's fired up, that's for damn sure." Zoe smirked.

He looked over at his other sister, then opened his arms wide and pulled them in close to his sides. "I've missed you girls."

"Don't start mingling with the enemy," Evie called over to them from the loveseat. Drake eyed his middle sister. She had obviously had one too many margaritas and was feeling no pain.

"Why am I the enemy?" Drake asked reasonably.

"This is an inter-inter-mentionables," Evie finished. Yep, she was three sheets to the wind. Wilma took her margarita glass out of her hand. "Enough for you, young lady."

"Can I call you Mom?" Evie asked.

"I want you all to call me Mom," Wilma said. "I told you, I'm adopting every last one of you cantankerous Averys."

"He can't call you Mom. At least not yet." Maddie stabbed a finger his way.

What the hell?

"What'd I do?"

"I've heard Dare sing, it's not good," Evie lamented. "You can't have us do Karaoke."

He turned to Chloe who was now giggling. "What is she talking about?"

Chloe kept giggling. He turned to Zoe. "Well?"

"You're being overbearing."

"What do you mean by that?"

"You know." She got up and went over to the pitcher of margaritas on the dining room table.

"Karen, help me out." She just continued to play with her straw. She was so not a help.

"Trenda, you're usually a voice of reason. Tell me why everybody's acting crazy."

Zoe jumped up off the couch and rounded on him. She shoved her finger into his chest. "Don't you dare call us crazy. You're the crazy one. Did you or did you not tell the caterer that there had to be Denny's like options for some of the people."

"Well yeah. One of my buddies said that sometimes wedding food got too fancy, and he wished that the food was more like Denny's. I just wanted some Denny's options, but it's not like all the food will be like Denny's," Drake defended himself.

"What the hell were they going to do, have a short order cook, serve up a damn Grand Slam breakfast?" Zoe growled.

"How'd you find out about that anyway?" he asked Zoe suspiciously.

"Don't forget about the florist," Trenda called out helpfully.

Drake winced when Chloe hit him in the arm that had almost finished healing. "What was that for?"

"Did you really ask for them to add in magnolias? Five days before the wedding?"

"Why are you poking me?"

"Because nobody does that. You ask the bride what she wants. Flowers are sacred to the bride. What's more magnolias are out of season, you big dolt."

Drake stood. "Look, I can deal with Neanderthal. But I draw the line at oaf and dolt. Got it?" He heard Wilma giggle behind him.

"If the clown shoe fits," Evie quipped.

Piper slipped in front of him and wrapped her arms around him. Then she turned to her other sisters. "You need to back off. You know his intentions are good."

"I refuse to have to soak my feet in vinegar for two days because he has misplaced good intentions," Chloe stated firmly.

"Drake, Honey, did the florist get back to you on the cost of the magnolias?" Wilma asked.

"No."

"Check your phone, you and Karen were both copied on the cost."

Drake pulled out his phone and scrolled through his e-mails. He blanched. "Is this a joke?"

"They're out of season and have to be shipped in from a hothouse. It's not a joke," Karen finally spoke up.

"You had a magnolia tree in your yard back in Tennessee, I know you liked it."

"I want red and cream roses in my bouquet," she said quietly.

Fuck, he was a dolt. And an oaf.

He walked over to her, and pulled the empty glass out of her hands. "I'm so sorry. I think I might have gone a little overboard." He ignored the laughter behind him.

She sighed. Shit, she wasn't even giving him the pass of, 'you were just trying to help'. He was totally in trouble.

"What can I do to make this better?"

"Nothing!" at least four of his sisters shouted simultaneously.

"I want you to have the flowers you want," he whispered quietly.

"I don't want Grand Slam breakfasts either."

"Or Dare singing Karaoke," Evie called out.

Drake threw up his hands. "I'm tapping out."

"Thank Jesus," Trenda said.

"Now that he's ousht of it. I haf something to tell you." Drake winced. Thank God Aiden was going to be the one to handle the hammered Evie.

"What?" Karen asked.

"We, the SEAL Sisters..." Evie waved her hand, "not the Avery Sisters, have a couple of things up our sleeves. Your flowers, *without* magnolias, have been taken care of. As a matter of fax, fax, fact all decorations are taken care of. And..." Evie waved her hand again with a flourish, "...there is a place for a band, dancing, and *no* place for a short order cook. Sophia is managing the caterers and the wait staff."

"We don't have a band," Drake protested. "I found a good DJ. He mostly does Bar Mitzvahs, but he's done a couple of weddings. I gave him a playlist."

The women groaned.

"What?"

"Did you provide him with anything but classic rock and country music?" Zoe demanded.

"What else is there?"

"The SEAL sisters have it covered. Billy Anderson, Sophia's brother was able to get a really good band to come and play. They do gigs from LA to San Diego. What cinched it was the two days they could spend on Catalina scuba diving after the wedding reception."

Drake saw Karen's eyes light up and he relaxed. That's all he'd wanted when he got involved. Karen happy. He pulled her hand to his lips and kissed her palm.

"Are we good?" she asked.

"I don't know, are we?"

"I want to marry you with all my heart," she said softly. Could he be any luckier?

"I love you more." He pressed his lips to hers. "Mmmm, chocolate." She laughed.

He sauntered out the door to go back to Clint's house. He still had one surprise left.

HE SLIPPED behind Karen as she stood at the sink and kissed the back of her neck. "Little Man is out like a light."

"That's what happens when you keep him fat and happy," she said warmly as she handed him a pot to put into the dishwasher.

"Are we okay?"

"Why wouldn't we be?" she asked in surprise.

"Because I screwed up."

"I think we can agree that in the screw-up department we've both earned points in the last few weeks," she said wryly. "Hand me those glasses, will you?" Drake picked up the two wine glasses from the island and she dunked them in the sudsy water. He rested his chin on her shoulder, and watched her wash the goblets.

"Yeah, but if we are completely honest, mine was kind of normal for me. I might could do it again."

"Yeah, you might could," she teased. "Are you fixin' to?" she asked with a drawl.

"I love it when you talk southern." He blew in her ear. "And no, I'm not fixin' to. But I do love to fix things, especially where you're concerned."

Karen rinsed her hands and dried them. She turned to look at Drake. "I know you do. I find that trait endearing, but you know you don't have to, don't you?"

"I don't know if I can stop." He thought about his conversation with Finn. His friend had needed to be confronted, not just because it was the elephant in the room, but he knew deep in his heart it was that last little bit that would make him totally welcome. The fact that someone wouldn't tip-toe around the subject. Yep, he needed to fix things. Granted, sometimes he fucked up...

"What are you thinking so hard about?"

"That Piper is over at Evie's. That your mom and Andrew are asleep, and we have some time to practice creative sex time."

"First we have to finish the dishes."

"Two people will make this go faster," he said. He gazed down at her full lower lip and then took a gentle bite. She moaned and wrapped her arms around his neck.

"The dishes can wait," she said softly.

"I was hoping you might see things my way."

12

———————

THE PACIFIC OCEAN OFF THE COAST OF CALIFORNIA WAS SO different than off the coast of Alaska. Even in December it was gorgeous, bright, and it was going to be warm. The forecast said it would be in the mid-seventies tomorrow for the wedding. Karen was over the moon. For so many reasons.

"Look Andrew, can you see the casino?" The island of Catalina was looming large in front of them as the boat came closer. It looked like something you would see on the Mediterranean Coast. The palm trees and homes climbed the cliff side, with the spectacular circular red casino gracing the harbor with all the boats and their white sails soaring upwards. As a matter of fact, it was like being in California's version of Monte Carlo.

But as charming as Avalon was, Two Harbors was even better, at least in a SEAL's opinion, and in hers. The twenty or so guests who weren't family or part of the military contingent would be staying in Avalon, and then take a boat over tomorrow afternoon to Two Harbors for the wedding and reception. Drake and Karen had arranged a boat to take them back to Avalon at midnight.

Gray and Mason had arranged for the teams to have two days off. There was snorkeling, scuba diving, mountain biking and kayaking that they would indulge in the day after the wedding.

Andrew gurgled as she held him up.

"Are you ready for the big day?"

He shoved his fist up the air. She knocked hers gently against his in a mini fist bump. He smiled. It wasn't gas. Her son knew how to smile, even if he was only six weeks old. She turned around and saw Zarek smiling at her with his arm around Chloe. He swore he hadn't drawn the short straw, but she kind of thought he and Finn had. They were the guys who came over a day early with Karen, Drake's sisters, and her Mom. They had booked one of the two lodges on Two Harbors. It was the second town on the other side of the island from Avalon.

"Auntie Karen, I'm gonna throwed the flowers liked I did for Auntie Evie and Auntie Chloe. Only I'm going to do it better this time. I's practiced now."

Karen looked down at Bella and smiled. She'd been to Evie's wedding, not Chloe's. God knew what was going to happen now that Bella had practiced. She had handed rose petals to the audience members in Evie's wedding, which resulted in a lot of laughter. Maddie had taped the event so Drake and she could see Chloe's wedding, so Karen had seen Bella's performance. She had literally done twirls, which resulted in the basket spewing petals all over the crowd. Karen thought about asking what kind of practicing she had done, but truly, she wanted to be surprised.

"When are you going to start T-Ball?" Finn asked the

little girl. "From what I hear you have the arm to be a center fielder."

Bella's face scrunched up, but then she brightened. "I'm going to be a quarterback."

"Damn right," Evie yelled. "None of that T-Ball shit. You go for the gusto." Evie opened her purse before her niece could say anything and handed her a dollar for swearing. Bella grinned.

Trenda wandered over to where they were all standing. "Quarterback huh? I think a little girl I know will have to start working some vegetables into her diet along with chocolate if she wants to be quarterback for the Volunteers. But you do realize their uniforms are orange, don't you?"

Bella's face scrunched up again. "Vegetables? Orange?" She looked up at Finn. "What's a center fella?"

Karen walked toward the front of the boat, laughing. She didn't want to miss a moment of the view as they headed around to Two Harbors. Her heart was beating a mile a minute. In less than thirty-six hours she would be married to Drake. Every dream she'd ever had was coming true.

DRAKE HAD NEVER MET Karen's brothers or father before. He'd called her dad when he asked for permission to marry her. Not that he was going to take no for an answer. That had been Mason's idea. It had been an interesting call. Turned out James Eastman was a man after his own heart. Drake still remembered how the man had explained Karen was his little girl and he understood that Drake was a Navy SEAL, so he couldn't take him in a fair fight, but he was more than willing to hire out a contract on Drake if he ever hurt his daughter. Yep, Drake liked the old guy.

All the Eastman men flew in that afternoon. None of her brothers were married. Jim, the eldest, was the sheriff of a small town outside of Kenai where they were born. Alex, the middle son co-owned a lumber yard, and Leif the youngest worked for the Forestry Department. According to Karen, Leif spent a good deal of his time doing search and rescue and policing illegal hunting.

He had invited the four men over to his house for a barbeque. They had flown into San Diego at one o'clock, and everyone was going to take the early morning boat ride to Catalina in the morning. This was a chance for them to get to know one another before the wedding. Drake had invited his team, and some of the Black Dawn team, since they were coming to the wedding as well.

Jack was bringing the steaks since the good butcher was near his house. He'd forced money on him at the base yesterday, it had been tough. He knew the fucker was going to use the money to buy some kind of wedding present, but at least he'd tried. Then there was Aiden, he made him get the booze because he was such a picky bastard about what he liked to drink. Since he was officially family he'd given up trying to foist money on him. Drake made sure there was every kind of beer imaginable for the eclectic tastes of his friends. It had taken him damn near an hour to find every single brand. He'd even found out from Karen the kind her brothers and Dad drank. It was an Alaskan brand called Berserker. He bought extra, because he knew all the guys would be wanting to try it because of the name.

Drake was firing up the grill when he heard someone beating on his front door.

"Let yourself in," he yelled.

"Can't. Open up."

He jogged to the front door when he heard Mason's

voice. Opening the door, he laughed at what he saw. Mason was holding at least eight pastry boxes. "I thought Sophia was on the island."

"She baked yesterday."

"Hey wait, did you kick my door?" Drake peered down at the scuff marks on his door.

"They'll wash off, Billy does it all the time."

"Where's Billy?"

"He's behind me with the bowls of potato and macaroni salad."

Drake rubbed his hands together. "Love it, no cooking, only grilling."

"Potatoes and corn?"

"Already on the grill." Drake grinned. "They'll come off when the steaks arrive."

Mason headed to the dining room table. "You nervous?"

Drake looked around and saw Billy still hadn't made it through the door. "Maybe a little. Actually, went to three different stores to find the beer they like. Couldn't believe I did that."

"Yep, you're trying to make a good impression. It's a red letter day."

"She's worth it. I want her to be happy. She adores her dad and brothers."

"Her mother thinks the world of you," Mason reminded him.

"It's not the same as the men. They'll have a whole different yardstick. Remember, I hated Aiden."

"You liked Zarek."

"He did wonders for Chloe. What wasn't to like?"

Mason just shook his head. "Have a brownie and a beer it'll take the edge off." He pulled a thickly iced piece of chocolate goodness out of one of the boxes, and Drake took it and went to the fridge. He opted for milk. There was no way he was going to screw with the heaven that was Sophia's fudge brownies by drinking anything but milk.

"Can I have a glass?" Billy asked.

Drake grinned when he saw that the young man had three brownies in his hand. "You know you should save some for the other guests."

"You're kidding right? Sophia made about eighty. Then she made apple brown betty, cherry pie and because it's December she said there had to be pumpkin pie."

"What the hell? I thought she was making stuff for the wedding?"

"She did. Remember she has two employees now. My sister is the shiznit. She cranked." Drake snatched two of the brownies from Billy's hand. "Go grab more while I pour you some milk."

Billy grinned. Drake was in the midst of pouring milk when Finn and Dare walked in the front door with Wyatt Leeds. Drake was not surprised to hear Wyatt running his mouth.

"You didn't eat those," Billy nodded towards the untouched brownies.

"I was just messing with you. Actually, I'm looking forward to the steak, potatoes and pumpkin pie."

Billy picked up his milk and started drinking. He was staring at Drake, and he could tell the kid had something on his mind. "Spill it."

Billy put his now empty glass on the counter and took a surreptitious look around the room. Satisfied that they were alone, he cleared his throat. "It was a good thing what you and Karen did, giving your son Mason as a middle name." Billy's eyes were suspiciously bright. Damn, Sophia's miscarriage and fertility issues had been hard on even Billy.

"Billy, there's something you need to understand. We did this because Mason is my brother, maybe not by blood, but by every other standard, he's the man who is my kin. Between you and me, after the wedding Karen and I plan to ask them to be Andrew's Godparents."

"That's righteous."

Drake laughed. "Schiznit. Righteous. You really are a surfer, aren't you?"

"Southern California born and raised," Billy said proudly.

Drake rolled his eyes.

"What's so funny?" Mason asked.

"You surfer dudes," Drake said. "That's what's funny."

"You surf now," Mason said.

"He *kind of* surfs," Bill qualified.

"We need to get you two deer hunting," Drake said laying on his Southern accent.

"Now you're talking," Jack said holding armfuls of beef wrapped in white butcher paper. "We need to take them to Texas and get them hunting. My stepdaddy would love to host them at the ranch."

"That goes out on the deck," Drake said pointing at the steaks. "Follow me."

He had the steaks grilling when Clint clapped him on the shoulder. "Your future in-laws just arrived. You better go greet them. I'll take over your grilling duties."

Where Wilma and Karen were redheads, the Eastman men were all big blond-haired Vikings. Hell, one of the men was a little bigger than he was.

"Drake!" James Eastman shouted, his smile broad. Well that was a good sign. What wasn't a good sign was that none of the three younger men standing behind him were smiling. Fuck 'em.

"Hey James, glad you could make it." He held out his hand.

James Eastman stepped forward, his limp barely noticeable. "I like your place," he said as he shook Drake's hand.

"Can I get you something? Karen told me you drink Berserker, so I have some of that on hand."

"Well that's mighty nice of you, isn't it?" He turned to look at his sons. When he saw their blank expressions, he scowled. "What's your problem?"

"Besides the fact that he got Karen pregnant before marrying her?"

Drake would bet anything that was the sheriff. He was in his face before he was finished speaking. "That sounds like you're saying something against your sister. Are you?" Drake growled.

"Absolutely not," the man growled back. "My sister is a kindergarten teacher. You're a fucking sailor."

"I didn't notice your ass coming down here before you were officially invited. Doesn't seem to me like you were all that concerned."

"You absolute—"

"Enough!" Mason and James Eastman shouted at the same moment. Drake and Jim continued to stare at one another.

"Drake, Karen begged my wife to keep the pregnancy from her brothers. It wasn't until the baby was born that they found out about their nephew."

Drake and Jim ignored Mr. Eastman. Instead the sheriff continued to talk. "You forced her to give up her teaching career, sell her house and move across the country to where she had no friends, family or support system when she most needed one. You don't fucking deserve her."

"Here, here! Can I take the first swing?"

Fucking Aiden.

The Vikings all turned around and basically saw one of their own when they looked at Aiden O'Malley. "Who the hell are you?" Jim Eastman demanded.

"His brother-in-law. The man who had the gall to marry one of his six younger sisters. I've had to endure so much crap from this man that it's a wonder I didn't end up growing a tree out of my ass."

Drake heard snickering from behind him. He was pretty sure it was Billy and Wyatt.

"If he has six younger sisters, then he's a royal dick for doing our sister dirty," the giant blond said.

"They grow 'em big up in Alaska, don't they Mason?" Aiden commented.

"Seem to," Mason agreed.

"What's your name?"

"Leif Eastman."

Aiden held out his hand. "I'm Aiden O'Malley. I married Drake's middle sister Evie. I totally fucked up with her. She ended up taking a vacation in Turkey and got kidnapped. It was my fault. Drake would have been within his rights to pour gasoline on me and light a match."

"You fuck up with Evie, and I'll still do it," Drake muttered.

"See why I want the first swing?" Aiden said.

"Stay the fuck out of this O'Malley."

"I can't. Unfortunately, Evie would have my ass if you didn't show up at the wedding because you were dead, or even worse, you showed up with a black eye and a broken nose. Apparently, these women set store in wedding pictures."

"Stay. Out. Of. It."

"Shut it, you oaf."

Drake took a step toward Aiden. "I am so sick of being called an oaf."

"Did you or did you not dye my wife's foot red?"

A loud whistle pierced the air.

Drake and Aiden stared at the one Eastman brother who hadn't spoken. "Are you two done?" he asked.

Aiden smiled. "It depends, what's your name?"

"I'm Alex. Apparently, I'm going to be the voice of reason tonight. Drake, did I hear you bought Berserker for us?"

"Yeah," Drake said suspiciously.

"Are you the father of the handsome nephew that now has my phone's memory almost at capacity?"

Drake grinned proudly. "Yep."

"Jim. Leif. Back the fuck off. Karen is happy. We're uncles. And I want a beer to toast Andrew."

13

Karen woke up rested and refreshed. Drake had arranged for Trenda and Evie to each take a feeding shift with Andrew with some frozen breast milk. What a boy scout. Okay, maybe not a boy scout, but he sure was a sneaky planner. Hers was the only room with a bathroom connected, the rest were sharing bathrooms. She could hear the sisters laughing in the hallway.

Karen watched with a grin when the doorknob started turning. She had a bet that it was Bella, and when the dark curly head peeked in, she mentally won extra bacon with her breakfast.

"She's awake!" Bella screeched. "She's awake!"

"Well if she wasn't, she is now."

Maddie tousled her niece's hair as she walked in with Andrew. "I've got niece and nephew duty during breakfast."

"How'd that happen?"

"This isn't going to happen for me again for a while. So, I need to take advantage."

Karen sat up in bed and fluffed her pillows behind her.

"You're finishing your master's program at the end of the school year, aren't you?"

Maddie crouched down when Bella tugged on her sleeve. "Yeah, I'll be done."

"So, have you considered moving out to California? I know for a fact that Evie has told you she wants you to stay with her and Aiden for a bit."

Bella placed a delicate kiss on Andrew's forehead. Could she be any sweeter?

"Right now, California is out of the picture."

"Why?"

"It's complicated." Maddie stood up. "Come on, Sweet pea. Do you want to help me feed Andrew his bottle?"

"Oh, I can handle this feeding. Bring him here." Karen held out her arms. "You feed Bella, and I'll get Andrew fed. Then you can take over while I eat. Is it a deal?"

Maddie gave her a thoughtful look, but then nodded. "Deal."

"I want a deal." Bella smiled. "Where's my deal?"

"You get breakfast with me. I think they have chocolate croissants."

Bella jumped up and down. "That's my deal, all right. Where are they?"

Karen laughed, and Maddie handed over Andrew. "Follow me, Miss Bella, and I'll take you to your yummy breakfast. But you have to eat your eggs and fruit too."

"But I still get chocolate crows, right?"

"Right." Maddie winked at Karen and guided Bella out of her room.

Andrew blinked lazily up at her. "Are you excited for the big day?" Karen adjusted her nightgown so that Andrew could help himself, and he did. "Dig in. I need to fit into the dress, and there isn't a lot of wiggle room in the bust."

Karen started humming the song that she knew would be playing during the wedding. It was going to be a surprise to Drake. He'd actually heard it once, and asked her who was singing. High praise from a man who thought that Toby Keith and Lynyrd Skynyrd were the end all be all.

The ceremony wasn't due to start until three o'clock. Looking at the antique clock on the wall, that was eight hours from now. It was going to be both the fastest and slowest eight hours of her life. There was so much to get done she didn't know how she could manage it all in such a short amount of time. But then there was the fact that eight hours seemed like an eternity to wait to finally be fully committed to Drake.

Andrew shook his head. She was holding him too tightly.

"I'm sorry, Honey. Mama wasn't paying attention, was she?" She lifted him to her other breast. Three more hours and the boat would dock. Drake and the men would arrive with the SEAL sisters, the caterers, wait staff and band. The set-up for the wedding was being handled by folks over from Avalon, and they would be coming via bus.

She sat up straighter. Holy hell, they'd figured out the band for the reception, but how were they handling the music for the wedding? Dammit, she wanted that song playing. She had a whole list of songs she wanted played for the wedding. How could she not have thought of this? She'd been so focused on the music for the reception.

"Knock, knock."

The door opened, and Evie's face appeared.

"Uh-oh. This doesn't look like the happy bride. This looks like the stressed-out bride. What, did you find a pimple?"

Evie was shoved from behind and Trenda followed her

into the room. "Don't pay any attention to her. You look beautiful. But we felt a disturbance in the force."

"I felt a disturbance, you wanted to play with Andrew," Evie corrected her sister.

"Whatever. We're here now. What's wrong?" Trenda asked.

"The music."

Karen felt herself hyperventilating. Andrew unlatched and pushed against her breast. He let out a yell. It was like he was psychically connected to her. Breathe Eastman. Breathe. Wait, she was going to be Avery. Just thinking that, calmed her. She was going to be Karen Avery tonight.

"She's gone."

"Totally. Off in la-la-land."

"What?"

"You're thinking sexy thoughts about our brother." Trenda smirked.

"Carnal thoughts. She's definitely thinking wedding night thoughts," Evie corrected.

"Damned C-Section." Karen sighed. "That's still off the table." Shit, had she said that out loud? To Drake's sisters?

Evie and Trenda laughed. "I love how her blush clashes with her red hair," Trenda said to Evie.

"Stop it you two. Focus. The problem is the music. I have a thumb drive of the music I want played for the wedding itself. I forgot we weren't having a DJ, and I don't know what kind of sound system we have, and I don't know who's in charge," her voice trailed off.

"Where's the thumb drive?" Trenda asked.

"In my purse. In the side zippered compartment." Karen waved her hand towards the dresser.

Evie went over to her bag and pulled it out. "Got it."

"Yeah, but what are you going to do with it?" Karen questioned.

"Give it to Lydia. She's got your six. Don't worry."

"Six?" Trenda asked.

"She's got you covered. She's watching her back. It's like the number six on the clock and you're at twelve," Evie explained.

She smiled. "Got it. Are you sure Lydia can fix this?" Karen asked.

"Honey, trust me, there's nothing to fix. I'm just stunned Lydia hadn't asked you for this before now. Are you sure you didn't tell Drake about your song choices?"

Andrew was getting fussy, so she put him up on her shoulder to burp him. "No. I know I didn't. There's one song I wanted to surprise him with."

"Is it the Eagles?" Trenda asked.

"Nope."

"Steve Miller Band?" she guessed again.

"Give it up," Karen said smugly. "Are you sure Lydia can take care of this?" Please God say she hadn't screwed this up.

"If she can't, Clint can. Between the two of them, they could tap into the Hubble telescope by breaking into a hardware store. They've got you covered," Evie assured her.

It was true. How often had Drake bragged about Clint? And Lydia was no slouch. As soon as she sighed with relief Andrew settled down and let out a huge belch. Karen and the two sisters laughed.

"He's his father's son," Trenda said. "Now give him to me, so you can go have breakfast."

Karen reluctantly passed Andrew off to his aunt.

"We have you covered," Evie said, tossing the thumb drive up in the air, then catching it. The girl was a nut. "The twins are just getting up, so hustle up before the foods all gone."

Karen threw back the covers and hopped out of bed. God, it felt good to feel good. Not a twinge of pain. It wasn't fair that sex, real sex, was still off the table.

"We'll leave you to it."

Karen watched as Trenda nuzzled Andrew's neck.

"I get to hold him next," Evie was saying as they left the room. How much longer before she and Aiden had one of their own?

Karen went over to the bed she'd just vacated and grabbed the pillow to hug, and then tossed it back on the bed in disappointment. Damn, it didn't smell like Drake.

THANK GOD FOR SOPHIA, Lydia, Beth, Rylie and Angie, Miranda, and Kenna, except for them, Drake felt like he was on a mission. Could he be surrounded by more testosterone? What was worse, they were all giving him shit. Except, of course, for the Eastman brothers. They were still looking at him like he'd crawled out from under a rock. Especially Leif.

He watched as James Eastman left the circle of his sons and came to approach him.

"Karen loves you, she's made that clear enough. But my wife. Somehow you have her convinced that you're perfect for our daughter, and she doesn't give her seal of approval to just anyone."

Drake waited.

"Wilma will work on the boys, they'll come around. You'll see."

Drake didn't really care, except for the fact that Karen would.

"And you?"

"You asked for permission to marry her. That showed class. I also trust my wife's instincts. In forty years I haven't known her to be wrong." James paused and looked him dead in the eye. "But the first time you fuck up with Karen, Jim will shoot, Alex will put your body through a band saw, and Leif will feed your remains to a bear."

Drake snorted. "Points for creativity. I like it."

James patted him on the back and walked back to his sons. Drake saw that his limp was a little more pronounced on the rocking boat. He admired the man. Karen said that even with the prosthesis he still went downhill skiing with his sons, apparently, he hadn't let the cancer beat him.

"Getting some advice from your father-in-law?" Finn asked.

"Not hardly." Drake grinned.

"Like that, huh? Well I can give you a few pointers if you want."

Drake stared down at his friend. "And just what do you think you have to offer?"

"A small piece of advice. Something that I had to learn the hard way."

Now this would be worth listening to. "I'm listening."

"Relax into the moment. Don't think of the past, don't wander into the future, treat the present as the gift it truly is. Cherish every second as it's occurring. I know you. You'll only ever have one wedding day. Breathe it in."

Drake opened his mouth to make a smartass comment, then shut it. Finn's eyes twinkled.

"Bastard. When'd you get to be so smart?"

"Dumbass, I was always smarter than you." Finn grinned. "I got the girl first, didn't I?" They looked through the plexiglass at the women who were seated on the inside of the boat.

"Angie's been good for you."

"I could say the same about Karen. How is it being a father?"

"Scary as hell. But the best thing that's ever happened in my life. Having Andrew has changed everything. That thing you said about staying in the present. It resonates. I keep worrying about the future, but if I do that, I'll miss the moments with him now. And I sure as hell don't want to miss any moments of this day with Karen." Then Drake glanced over at his future brothers-in-law. "Well maybe I can gloss over *some* moments."

"Bullshit, you were even worse to Aiden."

"Well he deserved it."

Finn laughed. "You're never going to change."

"I hope that's not true. I have a son to raise. I would hate to think I don't mature right along with the kid."

"If you feel that way, then there's hope for you yet."

They watched as Avalon came into view. Drake's excitement rose. This was it. This was the day he was claiming Karen as his wife. He couldn't wait.

———

"NUH-UH. Where do you think you're going?" Zoe and Chloe asked, their arms crossed. Bella looked up at her two aunts, then crossed her arms as well.

"I'm going to my room," Drake said.

"Karen's in there," Chloe countered.

"So?"

"You can't see her until she walks down the aisle," Zoe told him.

"That's ridiculous. Where am I going to put my stuff?" he hoisted his duffel bag and garment bag as he scowled at his sisters. Mason and Sophia walked past him, followed by the other couples of Midnight Delta.

"Hand it to me. Please tell me you didn't wad up your tux into the duffle bag," Zoe said.

Drake gave her the evil eye. Then turned so she could see the garment bag hanging down his back. "It's not a tux, they're my dress whites."

Zoe let out a low whistle. "I forgot. How in the hell did I forget that from Evie's wedding?"

"I love a man in uniform," Chloe said dreamily. "You know Zarek wears a uniform."

"Oh God, save me," Drake looked up at the sky.

"You go make yourself useful by helping with the set-up." Chloe pointed up the hill away from the lodge.

"Yeah," Bella said pointing in the same direction. Drake almost cracked a smile. Almost. He wanted to see Karen.

"Where's Andrew?"

"He's being doted on by his aunts. Go." Zoe pointed up the hill again.

Bella nodded.

Drake couldn't help it. He picked up Bella and tossed her up in the air. She squealed with pleasure. "Again! Again, Uncle Drake." Damn, she'd learned how to pronounce her 'R's.

"Can't, Lovebug, gotta go. You told me to, remember?"

"Can I go with him?" she asked her aunts.

"Sure you can. Drake, you two need to be back here by one o'clock."

"Then I get to see Karen?"

"No," the twins said in unison.

"You'll be getting ready in another room, then you'll go back to the hill where the wedding is taking place. Karen and the bridesmaids will be driven up in the golf carts. You manly men can hike it."

Drake turned and counted the number of golf carts. Hell, it was like they were at the La Jolla country club or something. "Are you sure there are enough?"

"Not quite, but we'll make do," Chloe said seriously.

"You're nuts."

"Can I drive a golf cart?" Bella asked. He looked down at his niece. She barely reached his knee, and she wanted to drive. He liked it.

"You can sit on my lap while I drive. I'll let you hold the steering wheel, how about that?"

"Yay!"

"DRAKE'S HERE. He's getting dressed."

Karen's stomach did a flip. She hadn't needed to be told. It was like she had internal Drake Avery radar. She had felt his presence fifteen minutes ago, and had known he'd arrived at the lodge.

Trenda walked into her room. "I'm going to kill my brother," she fumed.

"What now?" Zoe asked as she curled another lock of Karen's hair.

"I had to put Bella in the bathtub. She looked like she'd been rolling through a pig trough. How one little girl could get so dirty is beyond me. It's going to take half a bottle of conditioner to get out all of her tangles. You better be ready with a hell of a lot of hairspray and bobby pins, Zoe."

"On it." Zoe laughed.

Yep, they were definitely having more kids. Drake needed to have at least one daughter.

"Did someone take a picture of the site? I want to know what it looks like before I walk down the aisle."

She saw the five Avery sisters in the room look at one another.

"What?"

Evie left the crowded room and shouted for Lydia.

It took a couple of minutes and she walked in wearing a pale blue dress. She looked gorgeous with her dark skin and black hair.

Her eyes immediately started to water when she saw Karen. "*Dios mio*. You look beautiful."

"You're the beautiful one."

"Sorry Honey, the only beautiful woman on the day of a wedding is the bride," Zoe said. "It's the law. However, Lydia does look all Hispanic Hot."

"Thanks. And you look all Southern Belle Bridesmaid Bountiful," Lydia returned.

The Avery girls laughed.

"Seriously though, you ladies rock those burgundy dresses. I really like the black patent leather shoes. They have style."

Karen thought she might swallow her tongue she started to laugh so hard.

"Oh shit, I forgot. What happened to the dyed shoes?" Lydia asked.

"We couldn't donate them, that would have been too mean to someone, so we had a ritual burial ceremony. We would have done the chant and dance and wished something special for Drake, but out of kindness for Karen, we didn't."

"You're good women," Lydia said. "I might have cursed him just a little bit. Maybe made him just a little bald."

"No. Not his hair. I love his hair. Maybe you could make him a uhmm, uhmmm." Karen thought, but couldn't come up with anything. "Nope, no curses. I love everything about him exactly as he is."

"There's no hope," Zoe said, shaking her head sadly.

"Drake deserves to be loved that much," Piper said quietly.

Zoe put down the curling iron and hugged her little sister. "I totally agree, Honey." She guided Piper over to Karen. "Karen if I haven't said it before, let me say it now. I adore my big brother, and I couldn't be happier that you have taken him into your life and heart."

"Zoe, you're going to make me ruin the make-up you just did," Karen cried.

"*Dios mio*. I need to go hug Beth," Lydia said.

"Not before you show me pictures of the site. I don't want to see it for the first time when I'm walking down the aisle. I want my focus to be on Drake."

Lydia handed Karen her phone. "Scroll through the photos."

What? This couldn't be real. She thumbed to the next photo and it only looked more beautiful. It wasn't possible. She zoomed through the next image and the next.

"Lydia, what is this?" Karen asked in amazement.

Lydia smile was huge. "We wanted to give you a wedding present. This was it."

"It looks like something out of a fairytale. How did you do it?"

"We had the whole set-up trucked over from Avalon. That's how you got the rose covered trellis, the drapery and the hanging arrangements of rose balls."

"Let me see. I've never seen a rose ball," Evie said.

Karen handed over the camera in a daze. She'd never seen anything more beautiful in her life. Even if she'd dreamed a perfect setting for her wedding, she couldn't have come up with this.

"Oh my God, those are beautiful. How many roses are in one of those?" Evie asked.

"They were Sophia's idea. There have to be at least fifty roses in each one," Lydia said.

"Wait a minute," Karen said. "Give me the phone back."

She looked. Yep. "The aisle has cream rose petals strewn all over it. It's absolutely gorgeous, but what about Bella? She has her heart set on throwing rose petals."

"Silly girl. Who do you think threw *those* rose petals?" Lydia laughed. "When Bella walks down the aisle, she'll be throwing red rose petals. She's pretty excited that she gets to throw twice in one day."

Karen sat back in the chair. She should have known that these women would have thought of the little girl. Every single one of them had their hearts in the right place.

"So, are we good?" Zoe asked.

"We're good." Karen smiled.

"Thank God, because I still have a lot more curls to put in, and it sounds like Miss Bella is going to require some time as well. Let's get a move on."

14

THE DAY WAS BEAUTIFUL. THE SKY WAS BLUE AND HE COULD see and smell the ocean. He was surrounded by family and friends. He was blessed. But all he could do was stare at his son in Mason's arms.

"It only seemed right that your son should stand up with you as well, after all, he's going to end up being the best man you'll ever know," his best man, Mason, had said right as they walked out under the trellis. Drake was positive that it had been Sophia who had found the little sailor suit that Andrew was wearing. He wondered whether Karen was in on this, but he'd bet she wasn't.

Mason held his little boy like a pro, and when Andrew's head bobbed, Drake was positive that he was nodding his approval at the events of the day. That was when the music started. Drake turned to look down the aisle and he saw little Bella. She was a ray of sunshine that couldn't be contained. This time instead of throwing the red rose petals overhand, she was practicing underhanded pitches and giggling as they rained down on her head and onto the carpet of cream colored petals below her. She was having so much fun as she danced down the aisle that everybody laughed with her. When she got to the end of the aisle she raced up at Drake.

"I saved some just for you," and pitched them up high. All his sisters and teammates laughed as red petals fluttered down his dress whites. He started to turn to glare at all of them, but then the wedding march started and everyone stood up.

Time literally stopped. It was just as Finn had said. Every single moment was encased in amber, as he got his first glimpse of Karen Marie. Her father walked slowly, and she literally drifted beside him in a long white silk gown that was made for a Hollywood movie starlet of a bygone era. She looked seductive and elegant.

Mine.

The drifting needed to stop, she needed to move faster. He took a breath, and focused on enjoying the moment. Could any woman look more beautiful?

"Drake?" she whispered as she finally arrived.

He mentally shook his head. James was holding her hand out to him. He'd been watching her eyes, and hadn't realized that she was beside him. Finally. He grasped her hand. Soft and warm. They fit, they always fit.

His lips touched hers, and the world melted away.

"Pssst. We're not to that part yet."

Evie. What was she doing here?

"Rings. You still need to do the rings," Evie said in a stage whisper.

He heard snickering. But beautiful dazed green eyes looked up at him and he really didn't give a shit if his friends and sisters were laughing. They could all jump in a lake for all he cared. Then the minister cleared his throat. Oh yeah, rings. Yeah right. Dammit, he wanted her wearing his ring.

"Rings," he whispered down to Karen. Then she saw her eyes turn determined. He liked that. Seemed that someone wanted him bagged and tagged too.

They turned back to the minister who was grinning. Drake turned to his best man. "I need the rings."

Mason smiled. "I don't have them." He held out Andrew, and there tied into the little sailor scarf were the wedding rings.

Karen leaned over and giggled. "Hey cute boy. You're adorable. Give Mommy and Daddy our rings, won't you?" She untied the scarf while Andrew gurgled up at her and retrieved the rings. She handed hers to Drake, and kept his.

The minister coughed, and Drake put his arm around Karen and turned them to face the man.

Solemnly, they exchanged the powerful gold symbols of love, and words that held meaning to him were uttered. He looked into Karen's eyes as he promised his devotion, his love, his loyalty, his very soul to her. Having her promise her heart into his keeping, under the eyes of God, damn near brought him to his knees.

The minister opened his mouth to speak, but before he could, Drake had one more thing to say.

"Karen, my last breath belongs to you."

A single tear slipped down her cheek, but that smile was still brighter than star shine.

"You may now kiss the bride."

For a half heartbeat he waited for Evie to speak. She didn't. He swept Karen into his arms. His wife. Halleluiah, his wife. For eternity. His wife.

"LADIES AND GENTLEMEN, May I introduce Mr. and Mrs. Drake Avery."

The first strains of the song started as shouting, clapping, and whistling began.

Her legs went weak. As if by magic, Drake gripped her tightly around the waist.

"I have you," he whispered into her ear.

"I know."

"It's going to be fine."

"I know," Karen repeated herself. She wanted to take Andrew from Mason, but she didn't know if she could hold him. Then it hit her, she was dizzy, and she knew the reason why, it was pure unadulterated joy.

"We did it. We finally did it," she whispered.

"Yeah, we did," Drake crooned in her ear. "I like your song choice, Baby."

"You do?" She listened as the singer said he fell in love every single day under the light of a thousand stars.

"It's true Karen, your heart could never grow old."

He made her melt. Every day, every minute, every moment, she melted deeper into his soul.

"I love you."

"Do you think they're going to leave?" Evie asked sotto voice.

"Shut it," Trenda hushed her sister.

"We should get going," Karen said to Drake.

"We can stay here all night, there's no rush," he whispered. He always had her back. No matter what she would always be able to depend on Drake. Her husband.

Her husband.

"Everybody's staring."

"Fuck 'em."

Karen wound her arms around Drake's neck and drew him down for another kiss. He deserved another kiss, and she desperately desired one. This moment was perfect. She needed a little bit more time here in her personal fairytale with her prince. There weren't stars, instead it was beautiful twilight, but under this bower of flowers it was her idea of heaven.

Karen felt something soft hit her cheek, then something fluttered over her forehead.

"You're pwetty," Bella cried.

She opened her eyes and saw Bella scooping up another handful of rose petals off the carpet. The photographer was bent low to get a picture of the little girl. People were whistling and clapping. She sank against Drake's white uniform.

"You okay?"

"Mmm mmm." She nodded into his chest. She felt like she was floating. She laughed when she heard his stomach grumble.

"I think someone's hungry." She grinned up at him.

"I think they have food at the reception."

"Is it far?"

"There's a golf cart with your name on it."

"What—?"

She was up off her feet and in his arms before she could finish the sentence. "Put me down."

"No."

"Right this instant."

They were being pelted with rose petals as they made their way down the aisle. Everyone seemed to think Bella's idea was brilliant and Drake's laughter just made it all the better. He deposited her into a golf cart as soon as they made it outside. She caught sight of her brother Alex as he waved at her. She hadn't even noticed any of her brothers before now.

"What about Andrew?"

"Mason's bringing him to the reception, don't worry little Mama."

They wound up and around the back of the wedding area, until they reached a plateau. Once again, she was dazzled. There were colorful Chinese lanterns hanging in the Live Oak trees that surrounded the dance floor and tables covered with black silk, red roses and delicate brass lanterns. The band was set up, and beginning to play a country ballad that she absolutely loved.

Drake helped her out of the golf cart, and Karen heard the low hum of other electric motors arriving. Bridesmaid after bridesmaid was escorted up to the reception area. Like a well-oiled machine, the Midnight Delta men were paired off with their women, an Avery sister was immediately met with either an Eastman brother or a single member of the Black Dawn team.

They didn't have a head table, they sat at rounds. After everyone was seated, the band asked for everyone's attention and Mason stood up at his table and looked over at Karen and Drake. Somehow, in a maneuver that Karen was still trying to wrap her head around, her big husband had somehow managed to plant her, her dress, and their son, on his lap like it was the most natural thing in the world. So that's how the photographer caught them when Mason decided to give his toast.

"I've known Drake since we met at BUD/S. Nothing stopped him then, and nothing stops him now. I am honored that he would ask me to be his best man. I consider him the brother I never had."

"Drake, you're the man who tells it like it is. Okay, a lot of times you insert your foot in your mouth while doing it, but you always get your point across. You have a heart as big as all outdoors, you always know when we need a helping hand, and you're there. Just like you were for your sisters, even when you couldn't be there with them in Tennessee. No matter the type of fight anyone is facing, be it on the battlefield or a battle of the heart, you have their six."

"My friend, they often talk about the mighty falling, and there is no one mightier than you, my brother."

"Here here," Clint shouted.

Mason continued. "We waited with baited breath, and it was with joy in our hearts that we saw you fall at Karen's feet. There is was no one worthier for you my friend. When we met her in Tennessee we were greeted by a schoolteacher who schooled you, but then we saw her fight fiercely for you and your family, never backing down, never giving up. We were amazed at her ability to be the perfect match for you, providing you the love, the care, and the slap upside the head that you so often need. Welcome to our SEAL Team family, Karen."

Applause burst out, as Karen burst into tears. She tried to jam her face into Drake's neck, but he was having none of that. He was laughing.

"He sure called that right, you sure as hell schooled me."

"Drake," she wailed.

"School me again."

She looked at him in confusion.

"Show me how you'd like to be kissed."

Karen cupped his jaw, and guided his lips to hers. "I want a Drake kiss."

"I can do that."

The applause melted away as she was swept into the magic that was her husband's passion.

"HE'S TOTALLY in love with you," her mother said as she took Andrew out of Karen's arms. She gave her mom a questioning look. Drake was near the band and he was staring at her. Heat suffused her entire being.

"You don't even hear me? Do you?"

"What?" she asked her mom.

"He totally missed Maddie and Leif dancing."

"So," Karen said.

"They're kind of making a spectacle."

Karen scanned the dance floor and when she saw them, she grinned. They totally were. Her big blond brother with the petite brunette sprite looked awesome together.

"Don't stare," Her mom cautioned. "Drake might notice."

"Nope, now he's talking to the lead singer." That was odd. The singer went to the microphone and looked at her.

"Will Mrs. Drake Avery please come to the dance floor." Drake was standing there, a huge smile on his face with his hand out. What the hell? She loved her man, but one of the things that she knew from the get go was that he didn't dance. He stood, she clung, they swayed. It worked for them.

"Karen?" her mom prompted. "I think Drake's asking you to dance."

Karen stood up and walked over to her grinning husband. As soon as he took her hand, the band started to play. Drake put his big hand at her waist and clasped her right hand in his left. He'd never done this before.

"You with me?" he asked.

"I think so," she said hesitantly.

"Let 'er rip," he called out to the band.

A deep blues beat started and Drake swung her into a smooth glide as a deep bass voice started singing.

"We're dancing." She looked up at him in wonder.

"You're not listening."

"How can I? We're dancing."

"Listen to the words, Karen." Then in a low rumble as he twirled her around under the stars he started singing along with the band.

"You're the best thing to ever happen to me."

She faltered, but he caught her, and glided her through the next steps, and kept right on singing into her ear. Oh my God, he was singing and dancing. Chills raced up and down her spine.

Finally, the song came to an end, and she drew his head down and whispered into her ear. "You got it wrong. So very wrong. You're my best thing."

Vaguely she heard people clapping again.

The band started a new song. She clasped her arms around his neck, and they started to sway. "Where'd you learn to dance?"

"I've been going over to Clint and Lydia's so often so that Lydia could teach me."

She kissed the bottom of his jaw. "Thank you for that." She took a deep breath, and then snuggled in, breathing in Drake and the warm moonlit night. She felt the gentle breeze coming from the ocean, it was perfect.

The dance floor filled around them. She smiled when Mason and Sophia danced past them on the right, then Darius and Rylie on the left, but she all out grinned when she saw young Billy Anderson dancing with a girl named Rebecca who had visited her once with Sophia while she had been on bedrest. Such a lovely teenager.

"What has you smiling so big?"

"Besides the fact that you made all my dreams come true?"

Drake kissed the tip of her nose. "Besides that."

"Being surrounded by our friends and family is wonderful. Did you see Piper talking to Edna and Lacey?"

"The two teachers from your old school in Tennessee?"

"Yep, they're still over at that far table under the oak tree talking. And Edna's the principal."

"They've been at it all night. Which is good, I think Wyatt's been trying to make a move on Piper," Drake frowned. "She's far too young."

She could see Leif and Maddie dancing behind Drake, once again you couldn't see a bit of light between them.

Drake lifted his head, and Karen was sure his instincts had somehow tuned into the couple. "Did you hear that?" he asked her.

"What?"

He maneuvered her to the edge of the dance floor. One hundred yards of guest tables separated them from the drop off towards the water. To the right was the forest of Live Oak trees where the lanterns hung. The moon shimmered over the ocean, she could see the stars gleam brightly, the sight was gorgeous. Bella gave a tired wave from her mother's arms. She looked ready to fall asleep. Karen waved back at the girl.

Mason and Sophia came up on her right. "You sensed it too?" Mason said looking over at Drake.

"Now I can hear it."

"What?" Sophia asked.

Drake and Mason both squinted into the darkness, as Darius and Rylie came up on her left side.

She saw Rylie was squinting as hard as the three men. She shared a look of bewilderment with Sophia. Finally, she saw a spec of black against the moon.

"Chopper," Dare said succinctly.

"Two," Mason corrected. "Both civilian. They wouldn't be doing tours at this time of night."

"Maybe they're dropping off or picking up tourists," Clint said as he joined the group. Karen did a quick scan and saw Lydia sitting with her sister Beth and Jack, they were all eating cake.

"Bullshit," Drake said. "They're coming to this side of the island not the Avalon side."

There was the distant *whump whump* of a helicopter.

The first helicopter was still a long way out over the ocean.

"Ladies, come with me, we're heading for the trees," Clint said.

"It's a thousand yards out, but coming in fast," Mason said.

Clint tugged at Karen's arm. "Come on, Karen."

"Seven hundred yards," Drake called out.

"Scope!" someone yelled.

Karen was on the ground before the word scope was finished being shouted, Drake's body was on top of hers. She could still see a little bit of the dance floor.

Pfft. Pfft. Pfft.

Those were shots.

Blood burst starkly red on Dare's white uniform. She saw his body buck from where he was covering Rylie. The first screams started. Both men and women.

"Down! Down! Down! Down!"

Pfft. Pfft. Pfft.

Andrew. She had to get to Andrew.

Karen heard glass shattering, then she heard the most horrifying sound of all, a baby crying.

"Andrew! Where's Andrew?" She shoved at Drake.

"Report on Andrew!" Drake roared, not getting up. Why wasn't he getting up?

whump whump

"Andrew's under a table with Karen's mom," Jack yelled.

"They're making a turn and the second one's coming. Get the civilians under the tables." Gray Tyler ran by her. "All of you, get your dress whites dirty. They targeted white, they want Navy." She saw he was wearing a blue suit and holding a gun. Why would he have a gun at a wedding?

Gray was bending over Darius, rolling him off Rylie.

"I'm fine," he gasped at his wife. "It's just a graze," he said as blood continued to pour from the wound from his shoulder. Or was it his chest? Karen couldn't tell.

"Fuck that shit. It is not." Karen watched as Rylie hiked up her skirt and pulled a gun from the holster that had been strapped to her thigh.

"Get me to Andrew." She shoved at Drake again, but he wouldn't budge.

"There's another one coming in. It's bigger," Gray yelled.

"Why is this happening? Why is this happening? Why is this happening?" The woman wouldn't shut up. Karen finally recognized her as Lacy, her friend and fellow teacher from Jasper Creek.

"Help Lacy," she said to Drake.

"Wyatt," he roared. "Help the little blonde teacher who's having a shit fit."

Above the crowd, she heard the young SEAL, say he was 'on it.'

"We've got to get the people off the dance floor and back to the trees for cover," Mason said.

"I'll take them," Rylie said. "You carry Darius." Her voice was tight.

Drake got up, helping Karen to a standing position, she

started to kick off her shoes. "Don't," he said. "Too much glass from the table lanterns." He bent down and ripped her dress from the hem to mid-thigh. "There, now you can move more easily. Follow Rylie, she'll take you to Andrew. Stay low. Get under one of the tables near the trees."

"Take off your jacket," Karen started tugging at his buttons.

"We'll take care of it. Trust us."

whump whump

whump whump

She needed to get to their son. "Andrew's under the table near the big tree there." He pointed.

Rylie, Sophia, and she started out as fast as they could. She stopped short when she saw the body of a white coated waiter. Rylie yanked her arm. "No time. Keep going."

Pfft. Pfft. Pfft. Pfft. Pfft. Pfft. Pfft. Pfft. Pfft.

The bullets were never ending. Dirt spit up to her left. Rylie continued to yank at her arm. Then Rylie stopped and planted her feet. She lifted her gun and shot upwards. Karen looked around in a daze and realized at least five men, including her brother Jim, were doing the same thing.

Andrew squalled. That was what was important. She quit looking at the people with guns and ran towards her son, praying that somehow Drake and his team would save their baby.

15

ANDREW WAS CRYING. DRAKE SAW THE WHITE SATIN OF Karen's gown glowing like a beacon in the moonlight, she might as well have been wearing a bulls-eye.

"I've got the civilians, you handle Dare," Mason said.

"Roger," Drake told his lieutenant.

"Need a rifle," Jack shouted from one of the reception tables.

"On it," Finn shouted back. Drake couldn't remember seeing Finn in the crowd when he was on the dance floor, but he heard him clear as day, and his voice was coming from where the golf carts were parked. If anyone could put his hands on a rifle, he'd bet the farm on Finn Crandall.

"Aiden!" Drake shouted. Dare was going to die if they didn't get him help. It was as simple as that. Aiden skidded in the blood and landed on his knees. He hadn't been in the wedding party, so he wasn't in dress whites. He slammed his Sig Sauer pistol into Drake's hands. "If they get close, try to take out whoever you can," Aiden said.

"I know what to do." Drake grabbed the gun. "Save Dare."

"I know what to do." Aiden ripped open Dare's jacket, buttons flying. Drake saw that Aiden had grabbed a silk table cloth. He was on it. He took another look toward where Karen had run, he couldn't see her. Hopefully she was safe.

"Mommy!" he heard Bella cry out as wind from the second helicopter sprayed dirt into his eyes. He smelled smoke. Damn it! The candles from the lanterns! More screams broke out.

"Drake, help me carry him to the trees," Aiden yelled above the sound of the helicopter rotors.

They picked up Darius and started toward a spot Clint signaled toward. It was further back amongst the woods with a table leaned against the base of an Oak tree. Perfect cover. Where was his wife? Where was his son? They better be under something just as good.

As soon as they got Dare under cover, a muddy Clint pushed Drake onto the ground and poured a pitcher of water on him. "Roll."

Drake rolled in the dirt, muddying up his clothes, then he smeared mud on his face. He stood up holding Aiden's gun. He saw that Clint had one too.

For an instant, Drake wondered why this was happening at his wedding, then put all thoughts of that to the side. It didn't fucking matter. What mattered was keeping everybody alive, and killing the enemy. He looked up. The first helicopter was dipping low and coming in to take another pass. He clearly saw someone leaning out the side door of the helicopter. They had a rifle. Their pistols might not have the range and velocity to pierce through the glass and hit the pilot, but they could possibly hit this shooter.

"Look Mommy, there's a fire."

He pushed Bella's voice out of his consciousness and

took aim. He took three shots. Drake grunted with satisfaction as a man fell out of the helicopter and into the brush two hundred yards away from the reception area onto the knoll above the bandstand.

Immediately a rifle tip took its place, showing through the same door, and more bullets flew, aimed toward Drake. He and Clint ran, wanting the shooter to follow them, further away from Aiden and Dare, away from Karen, Andrew, Sophia, and Bella.

Bullets careened past Drake's ear as he zigged and zagged away from the reception area, further into the trees to the South. The helicopter zoomed past, shaking leaves from the trees as it whizzed by. It would be turning soon.

Drake heard bullets that weren't from the helicopter. He looked over at the reception area and realized that almost every light in every hanging lantern had been extinguished, which helped obscure the shooter's targets. But the two small fires that had started weren't helping.

"I don't get it. Why aren't they just killing everyone?" Clint asked.

He was right. The men of Midnight Delta were being targeted. "Maybe we're dealing with honorable terrorists?" Drake panted sarcastically.

"Let's hope they stay that way."

They'd been successful, the helicopter had followed them. They were now out of the woods and at the cliff that overlooked the ocean, the helicopters were going to have to bank wide to come back. Drake watched and saw that this time it was the larger one that was coming in first to take another pass at them. They had maybe four minutes if they were lucky.

The men headed back at a dead run, Drake scanned the area as soon as they cleared the trees. The dance floor was empty, but people were still crawling out from under the tables surrounding it. He wondered how many more were still cowering underneath others. If the gunmen decided to just shoot, they could penetrate those tables in a heartbeat. They needed to get those people into the woods. Then he saw Dalton, Dex, Griff, and Hunter lifting tables to check underneath. Apparently, the men from Black Dawn had thought the same thing.

"No! It's safer here!" Drake saw Wyatt struggling with Lacey. She was refusing to move out from underneath a table. What the fuck? He was about ready to wade in when he saw James Eastman helping Hunter move a table and then fall. His leg went right out from under him. Drake took off at a run. The table had fallen on whoever was beneath it, and James was now out of commission. What was worse, the man wasn't wearing his Tuxedo jacket, his white shirt was bright in the moonlight, he'd be mistaken for a SEAL. As Drake was running toward his father-in-law, he saw that Zarek and Alex each had a fire extinguisher and were working on putting out fires. Now there were three of the damn things.

"Gray!" Hunter yelled. "Need you."

Gray ran toward the falling table from the opposite direction.

James was still holding up part of the table, allowing one of the back-up singers and a member of the wait staff to crawl out. "Carol's still under there," the waiter said.

Drake caught the table just as James' strength let out. He heard the roar of the helicopter rotors.

"We've got Carol," Hunter said. "Get the old man to safety."

Drake realized James' prosthesis had partially disconnected. James was struggling to get it all the way off.

"It's okay. I'm just going to carry you," Drake explained.

"If I get this off, I can hop beside you," James said.

"No time," Drake said as he lifted him in a fireman's carry. He headed in the same direction he'd last seen Karen going. He prayed that he would find her and prove to himself that she was okay.

He felt the wind of the rotors, and then he heard the bullets. They were aiming for James' white shirt. He had to get a move on. Drake ran for all he was worth, heading for the first cover he could get to. Bullets sang out.

All of a sudden, Drake felt like he'd been shoved to the ground, but he knew it meant that James had been hit by a bullet. He pushed up on his knees, stumbled, tried again. James groaned.

"Got you," Hunter said, as he came up to Drake's side and helped him up.

"James!" Wilma shrieked as they got deeper into the trees. Hunter took James off his shoulders and gently lowered him to the ground.

"I'm good," James said pushing up on his elbows.

Drake looked, and couldn't see any blood.

"They shot my fake leg," James grinned and started pulling on the prosthesis. Drake didn't need to see the show. His eyes zeroed in on red hair off in the distance. Why wasn't she with her mother? As if she could feel his gaze on her, she looked up at him. She was holding Andrew, sitting at the base of a tree with Sophia and Piper. Again, she knew what he needed. She gave him a thumbs up, and he felt a huge sense of relief. He and Hunter headed back to the tables surrounding the dance floor.

As they were about to clear the tree line, Mason stopped them. "Everybody stays still until the next pass. Finn found a rifle, he's going to take a shot at the pilots."

Mason pointed to a spot further up from the band stand. It was the highest ground that there was, but still not higher than the trees. "He's in the brush up there on the knoll."

Drake stared, but couldn't see a damn thing. Finn had the scope hidden well.

"Where did he find a rifle?" Drake asked.

"Angie told me she'd noticed a locked gun cabinet at the lodge. He got it from there. She's pissed that he made her report to me." Mason chuckled grimly. "But she gave me the other rifle that he brought. I told her to find Jack and give it to him."

Drake would be amazed if she would be able to find him in the mass confusion in the woods. Then again, he'd seen Karen and Andrew, so maybe it was possible.

Mason might have called for everybody to stay still, but that didn't mean they were quiet. He could hear the civilians talking. Some were crying. That one woman, Lacy, was loud and hysterical, but at least she was somewhere behind him and not out near the tables. Thank God, they weren't in a situation that required silence.

Drake, Mason, and Hunter stood just out of sight and watched as the larger of the two Bell helicopters came in from the East and bank in a sharp turn. It wasn't the smaller one where he had killed the shooter, which is probably why the door opened and once again someone leaned out to take aim.

"Come on, Boss, let me take him," Drake pleaded, his gun at the ready.

"Negative. Wait for it."

"Is it even possible?" Hunter asked in all seriousness.

Mason and Drake grinned at him when the helicopter jerked. They heard the report of the rifle and saw the crack in the glass. It wasn't clear, but Drake would bet his last dollar it was a headshot. It would take a moment or two, but that helicopter was going to go down. It listed crazily. Then he heard another shot, and the helicopter burst into a fireball in the night sky.

"He must have hit the fuselage," Mason said.

Drake nodded. It was still far enough out that the burning craft wasn't going to land anywhere near the woods. Another thing that Finn would have taken into consideration. The helicopter that had been coming in behind, banked West, heading back toward the ocean.

"It's too much to hope for that they're leaving, right?" Hunter was grim.

"We're so not letting you play craps," Drake said. "But when they come back, this time we're taking someone alive. You get me? Find Jack, he has a rifle."

Hunter nodded.

"Drake, taking someone alive might not be possible," Mason said.

"Alive," Drake said through gritted teeth. "We were targeted in our home. We need to find out who did this and rain down fire so that this never happens again. Do you understand me, Mason?"

Mason's eyes turned dark. "You're right. Alive. Go talk to Finn."

Drake paused. "Sophia's with Karen, Andrew, and Piper." His voice trailed off.

"I'll check on all of them," Mason assured him.

Something loosened in his chest.

He took off at a dead run. He had a pretty good idea where the shots came from, before he got there, Finn stood up. He was cradling the Remington .30-06 in the crook of his arm.

"Good shooting, Tex," Drake complimented his friend.

"Angie's the Texan."

"You claim one, you end up becoming one by default." Drake grinned.

"They'll be back," Finn said with resignation.

Drake nodded in agreement. "I want to take someone alive. We need to find out who's behind this and make them writhe in hell and publicly set them on fire so everybody knows you don't fuck with our families."

Finn stared at him. Drake waited. He knew his friend had changed with all he'd gone through. What would he say?

"Draw and quarter them first," Finn said, his tone was bloodthirsty.

Drake held out his fist and Finn bumped it.

"Do you know where Angie is?"

"Mason told her to give the extra rifle to Jack," Drake said.

"Man's going to climb a tree. Mark my words. For such a big guy, he's half monkey."

"How are you going to get them to land?" Drake asked.

"Crash land. Tell Jack we're going after the tail rotor. That'll do the trick."

"Gotchya." Drake watched as Finn sank back into the tall grass and totally disappeared before his eyes.

"It's only been nine minutes," Sophia said.

"What?" Karen looked up at the pretty blonde huddled next to her.

"Since we've been sitting here. It's only been nine minutes since I called nine-one-one." She pointed to her phone display.

It took a moment for Karen to catch up. That was when she realized Sophia's slim purse was a cross-body and had been on her while she had been dancing. While Rylie had a gun, Sophia was a normal person and had a phone. There was no way it could have been just nine minutes, it had been an eternity.

"What did they say? Will they be here soon?"

"They're on their way. They said it would take them fifteen to twenty minutes, but—"

"But they'll die if they come here. The helicopters will shoot them like fish in a barrel," Piper said loudly.

How did she miss Sophia making that call? Andrew was still crying. That's how. The latest explosion had him screaming. Nothing made her heart break like when Andrew actually cried tears. What was worse is that off in the distance she could hear Bella crying. Yeah, Lacy was crying too, but that was just getting on her last nerve.

"You two holding up okay?" Evie asked as she squatted next to them. She had to raise her voice to be heard over Andrew.

"How's Dare?" She and Sophia asked at the same time.

A shadow passed over Evie's face. "The guys have to get rid of that last fucking chopper. Aiden's been on the phone with the ambulance from Avalon. Their ETA is ten minutes, but they can't drive into a firefight."

"I think I saw someone who was dead. Did I?" Karen asked Evie.

Evie nodded. "It was one of the waitstaff. He was wearing a white coat. Aiden thinks that the shooters are targeting Drake and the rest of the SEAL team in their dress whites. This guy was just a mistake."

Sophia was gripping her phone so tightly that Karen

thought it might shatter. "It was my idea that they wear white. I thought it would look nice," she whispered.

Karen juggled Andrew up onto her shoulder and put her other arm around Sophia. "It wasn't your fault." She could tell she wasn't getting through to the woman. She tried changing the subject. "Have you tried calling Billy?"

"He texted me. He and Rebecca are with Wyatt and your friend Lacy."

"Poor Billy. I can hear her from here," Karen said.

"How about everybody else?" Evie asked.

"I've texted all of the SEAL sisters and all of Drake's sisters are accounted for."

"I'm still looking for Rylie. I haven't found her. Who was she with, Sophia? I want to take her to Dare. Aiden has him tucked away far to the East," she said as she pointed.

"Lydia and Beth said she's searching for Dare, so she's probably running around like a crazy woman," Sophia said. "How about I help you to look for her?"

Karen didn't want Sophia to leave but Rylie needed to be with her husband.

Evie gave Sophia specific directions as to where Dare and Aiden were, and then she and Sophia left to search for Rylie.

Karen turned to look at Drake's youngest sister. "Piper, Mom is over there with Trenda and Bella. I saw Drake and Hunter carry Dad over. I know Mom gave me the signal that Dad was okay, but could you go check on him and report back? I would but not with Andrew." She didn't want to tell the girl that she couldn't bear the thought of parting with her son to go check, nor was she going to risk walking over the uneven ground in her shoes.

"Sure," Piper said. "I'll be right back."

Karen waited with baited breath until she was sure Piper

had made it safely to the other oak tree. Piper turned around and grinned at her and shot her a thumbs up. Then she picked up her niece for a cuddle.

Andrew realized that she wasn't paying attention to him and he let out another squall.

"I know, Baby Boy, you're not a happy camper, are you?" He was a hungry camper, is what he was. But there wasn't a chance in hell she was going to nurse while bullets were flying, her son was just going to have to wait. He continued to cry and for just a moment Karen wanted to join him. She was scared as hell for Dare. *Please God, don't let him die.* She still couldn't believe she had seen a dead body.

Andrew kept crying, real tears, and she felt herself heave.

No! Don't start. You are not going to be the first SEAL sister who falls apart. Be a Rylie. Be an Evie.

She would bet her bottom dollar that Angie had a gun strapped to her thigh too. She wasn't going to cry.

She pushed up from the tree, so she could stand. She teetered in her heels, she might not be able to walk, but she damn well could stand and sway.

"I've got you, Sweetheart. It's going to be okay. I promise. Daddy's going to stop the bad men."

She swayed back and forth, crooning to her son. A flash of yellow and peach went running by. Shit it was Rylie and Evie.

How many minutes had it been since Sophia had made the call? How much longer did they have to wait for the ambulance? When was this going to end?

whump whump

whump whump

She saw branches falling from the trees over to her right.

Pfft. Pfft. Pfft. Pfft. Pfft. Pfft. Pfft.

Karen lurched to the ground and covered Andrew with her body. Please say that a bullet couldn't pass through her and get to him.

A scream sounded. It was Lacey.

A shout.

Something hit her.

IT WAS KILLING HIM. He was dying inside. Mason, Clint, Jim, and all of Black Dawn were shooting at the helicopter to no avail. Three rifles were peeking out of the helicopter windows and shooting into the oak trees. Jack and Finn couldn't take any sort of shot because that would mean the helicopter would land on the people hiding in the trees. At this point, Drake could give a shit less if they took the enemy alive or not, he just wanted the helicopter taken out. He knew Finn and Jack would feel the same way.

The helicopter zoomed low over the dance floor then started up over the bandstand and further upward to the knoll where Finn was waiting. Drake saw the tail rotor shatter at the same time he heard the rifle shot. Then he saw Finn get up and start running towards them. The blades of the helicopter swung eerily close to Finn as he ran, and the chopper plummeted to the ground. Finn dove behind the bandstand.

The SEALs and Jim were running flat out towards Finn and the crashed helicopter. Drake heard shots. All of them dropped onto the floor of the dance floor.

Another shot fired.

"Winged him," Finn yelled.

They crawled on their bellies over the wooden floor, up over the bandstand, and disappeared into the grass.

"Stay down, Jim." Drake hissed.

When they got to the crash site, Finn had already pulled the wounded shooter out of the wreckage. "Pilot's dead, but there's another one who's hanging on in the back."

Drake didn't stay to find out anything more. He no longer cared about retribution, he needed to find out if Karen and Andrew were okay after the shots that had been fired into the trees.

He wasn't surprised to see most of the men right beside him. Hunter and Jim could take care of the two injured men, the rest of them needed to make sure their women were safe.

As he was running across the dance floor he heard sirens. People started pouring out from the woods. Piper was one of the first.

"Drake, come quick," she yelled above the pandemonium. He ran even faster, as if that were possible.

He knocked down a waiter who couldn't seem to figure out to go right or left. When he was within yards of his youngest sister she darted back to the trees and he followed her, soon he was past her. He made a beeline to the tree that Karen had taken shelter under. Drake saw Wilma huddled over Karen's prone body. Trenda was holding a screaming Andrew. His heart settled just a tiny bit as he heard his son's loud yells. His baby was alive.

Drake was on his knees beside Wilma before he even knew how it happened. Then he heard the best sound in the world.

"Let me up," his wife said crankily. "I'm fine."

"You are not fine. Your dress is torn, and I can already see the swelling on your back," Wilma said in the same cranky tone.

"Let me see Andrew right this second," Karen yelled.

Drake laughed with relief. He'd only run into it a few times, but that redheaded temper was a sight to behold.

"Don't laugh," Mother and daughter said at the same time.

He laughed harder. He thought he might cry he was so fucking thankful. Trenda knelt and handed him Andrew.

"Give him to me," Karen insisted.

"Not on your life, Honey. You stay down until the EMT's check you out."

"EMT's? It's over?" she asked shakily.

"It's over."

She tried to push up.

"I said stay down." He bent low, so that she could touch their son. He stroked back her hair, and looked into the emerald depths of her eyes. "Thank you for taking care of our boy."

"Thank you for saving us."

He captured her mouth in a tender kiss. "I love you, Mrs. Avery."

"God, I love you Drake."

16

"We want in," Gray said as his team followed him into a dingy warehouse in San Diego.

What the fuck? How the hell had they found them? Drake gave Clint a dark stare. Clint pointed over at Dex.

"You don't get a piece of this," Mason said to the lieutenant of the Black Dawn SEAL team. "You know as good as I do this is more than just a matter of us losing our commissions, this is prison time if we're caught."

Declan cleared his throat. "I resent that. Nobody's going to get caught."

"Is this the guy you told me about?" Gray asked Dex. "He doesn't look like much."

A man stepped up from behind Declan. "Allow me to introduce myself. My name is Carson, I work with Declan, and you're Grayson Tyler, do you want me to tell you what you had for dinner last night? You went to the same old bar in Lincoln Park and ordered fish 'n chips. You need to watch it; all that grease isn't good for your cholesterol."

Drake watched as Gray absorbed the man's words. Fucking Carson, always needed to show off.

"So now you know a little bit about my team," Declan said. "I figured you'd want in on this little operation."

"My wife could have been killed," Griffin Porter said heatedly. Drake remembered the man from a train wreck two years ago. He was quiet, but deadly. "There is no way I'm not in on this op."

"A lot of our women could have been killed," Jack said with his deep Texas accent. "They had no regard for our families."

"Do we know how they found us? Was it the pictures that were taken of Drake and me? Or was it the fucker from the CIA on the last mission?"

"Carson and I have been working together on this," Clint said.

Shit, that was a scary thought. Clint had probably pulled Lydia in too. The three of them could probably hack NORAD if they wanted to.

"It was Mason's face," Clint said. "Do you remember that surfing championship you won when you were seventeen? They cross-matched it to the picture they took in Cameroon."

"Who's they?" Mason asked in a deadly whisper.

"The Decault Group," Carson answered

"Anybody else have it?" Mason asked.

"Currently the Decault Group has the information up for auction. The bid is up to twelve million to know the personal information of Midnight Delta," Carson said.

"How many bidders?" Drake wanted to know.

"Only two stayed in the game once it got into the millions. You can guess who."

"ISIS," Mason said. "Do we have a name and a contact of who the bidder is?"

Clint grinned broadly. "As a matter of fact we do, Boss."

"The Boko Haram isn't funded well enough for twelve million," Gray said.

"Oh, but I can guess who is ponying up the other bid. We left some unfinished business last year," Mason said, his expression grim. "I just didn't think they knew it was us."

"The Lius," Finn said bitterly. "You think that the extended family in China has decided to come after us?"

"Yep," Mason said.

"Congratulations, Mason," Carson said. "You win the toy in the Cracker Jack box."

"Like we said, Black Dawn wants in," Gray reiterated.

"Like *I* said, you're keeping *your* hands clean," Mason said succinctly.

"Gentlemen," a blond man who stood with Declan held up his hands. "All of y'all are out of this. That's why we're here."

"And who are you? Are you going to tell me my brand of toilet paper?" Gray asked.

"I do a little bit of this and a little bit of that. The name is Hudson."

"That tells us shit." Gray was pissed. It was interesting to see.

Dex spoke up. "Are you Hudson Wells?"

Hudson nodded.

"Hold up, Lieutenant. I've heard of him, former Army Ranger. He made a name for himself. Pissed some people off. But ended up with the Bronze Star for Valor in Afghanistan."

"How do you know this shit?" Gray asked the man who was in charge of Black Dawn's information.

"I'm betting you're a Cottonelle man." Dex grinned at his lieutenant.

"Shut it." Gray turned to back to Hudson. "So, you're a

cleaner. And Declan, you have some operation called the Shadow Alliance, what the fuck are you going to do for Mason and his team?"

"Yeah, what the fuck are you going to do? Because I want in. I don't really give a shit about Gray. This was my fucking wedding. My wife of four fucking hours ended up in the ER. Dare almost died. I'm going to get my hands dirty."

"No, you're not," Mason's voice echoed through the warehouse. "None of you are going rogue. Declan and his team have four weeks. He's assured me he can take care of it in four week's time."

"No, you can't. That's impossible. You mean to tell me you're going to take down ISIS when nobody else has?" Drake said derisively.

"Jesus, Avery, you aren't listening. But what else is new?" Declan said impatiently. "Clint and Carson have the name of the sheikh who is bidding on behalf of ISIS. He's currently in Qatar."

"If you make an example out of him while he's in Qatar all hell with break loose," Gray said.

"I trust them, Gray. You need to. They'll get the message across and make sure there isn't an international incident," Mason said.

Hudson cracked his knuckles. "I'm looking forward to it."

"I get China," Carson grinned.

"You and *Noah* get the Lius," Declan corrected.

"Spoilsport," Carson grumbled.

"I'm going to be taking care of Kevin Decault myself," Declan said.

Drake itched. Mason saw it. Finn saw it. Hell everyone, even Declan saw it. "Sidebar," Declan said to the room in general. Then he gave Drake a chin tilt and the two of them wandered off next to an empty shipping container that stank.

"Drake, you've gotta trust me."

"I don't *gotta* do nothing." Everything that made him a man cried out for retribution. Demanded that *he* be the one to mete out justice.

"I'm going to make this fucker pay. I'm going to make sure that everybody knows you don't fuck with a SEAL's family, okay?"

"Not good enough. This was my wedding. I'm going on this mission with you."

Declan laughed. "How do you figure that, big guy?"

"Something happens to Kevvie Decault, I'll turn you in. So, unless you want to face a life behind bars, you better let me in on this op."

Declan really started laughing hard. "There isn't a chance in hell they'd ever be able to pin it on me. Not even with you pointing the authorities at me. Number two, Finn likes me, and you wouldn't want to hurt his delicate feelings. Number three, you want vengeance, and I can get it for you. You can't, and you want to know why?"

This Drake had to hear. "Why?"

"You have a wife of two days and a child of seven weeks who desperately need you. Now. They need you now, Drake. They don't need you away from them. Karen just went through a harrowing birth, and her wedding, albeit memorable, was less than stellar. You need to get your ass home to her, and plant it there. At least until the next real mission. You need to let someone have your back on this, Brother."

Drake thought about Karen's chalk white face. So white he could easily count the small smattering of freckles across her nose. She was waking up every time he rolled over in bed. The only reason she was okay with him leaving tonight was that her parents were sleeping in Piper's room. Piper, meanwhile, was staying over at Evie's house.

"Can you Drake? Can you really leave your wife for this? You know you can trust me."

"Can I?" Drake hated the desperation in his voice.

"You can. You can trust all of us. We're going to shut this shit down, so that everybody will know you don't fuck with a Navy SEAL's family."

Drake felt movement at his back. He sighed, and turned. It was Finn and Mason. "I suppose you agree with this cowboy?"

"I have one question." Finn jumped in. "Declan, will you and yours be able to sleep at night if you move forward with your plans?"

Declan's demeanor turned solemn. "Finn, your issue was never taking out Liu. That was taking out the trash, just like this will be. Your brand of justice is sanctioned by our government. The people who work with me have moved on. Our brand of justice is handled in the shadows, but it's just as pure, just as righteous."

Drake considered his words. He'd worked with Declan and the Shadow Alliance before, he knew he could trust them. He knew he was right, his place right now was with his family.

"Thank you." Drake held out his hand. "We'll owe you."

"No, you won't. We're just doing the right thing. Nothing more, nothing less." Then Declan gave an evil grin. "However, you might loan us Clint and Lydia some time."

DRAKE WALKED in the front door of his townhome at three

a.m. The only light on was the one over the stove. Andrew's feeding would have been over an hour and a half ago. He armed the security system and went to the refrigerator. Quietly he asked, "Can I get something for you, James?"

"You saw me here, did you?"

"I'd be a pretty shitty SEAL, if I didn't notice someone sitting in the dark in my own damn house."

"Well come sit down with me a spell," James said. "If you're having a slice of Wilma's cake, bring another for me."

Drake cut two slices, and got two glasses of milk to go with it. You couldn't have German chocolate cake without cold milk. He brought it out to the dark dining room. The thin scrap of the new moon shone through the window. The two men ate in silence.

"So, what kind of plan did you put into place?" James finally asked.

"I beg your pardon?"

"This is too damned important for bullshit. My daughter, my grandson, and the man I now consider my fourth son are in danger." James placed his fork precisely down beside his plate. Drake could see that he really wanted to throw it, and probably the plate, across the room. "Fuck that, you're not in danger, your lives are on the line. Now tell me what you've done to ensure your survival. I know you've done something. I want to know."

"No, you don't."

James sighed. "Yes, Drake I do, but..."

"But?"

"But, I also want to know that you've protected yourself so that this doesn't boomerang back on you. But you're a canny bastard. Your boss seems bright too. I figure you've come up with a plan that won't backfire. Now tell me."

"I can't."

James' hand shot out quick as lightening and grabbed Drake by the front of his shirt. "You can, and you will."

Seemed like the three apples didn't fall far from the tree.

"I'll send you proof after it's taken care of, will that do it for you?"

James released Drake's shirt, then smoothed it out. He gave a half smile. "That will do just fine."

EPILOGUE

KAREN HADN'T BEEN BORED ONCE ON THE TWO-HUNDRED-MILE drive from San Diego to Bakersfield. Her husband was funny, with a capital 'F'.

"Now where are we headed?" she asked as they passed the Bakersfield exits.

"You'll see," Drake said with a secretive smile.

"Drake, you're passing the place with the butter burger. It was featured on Diners, Drive-Ins and Dives. I looked up places I knew you'd like before we went on this road trip."

Karen noticed that he let off the gas a little bit. "Woman, I fall in love with you more each day, did you know that? But this trip is about you."

Karen crossed her arms over the truck's seatbelt. "That's bullcrap. This is our honeymoon, it's about both of us."

Drake reached over and tugged one of her hands loose and rested it against his warm thigh, tangling their fingers together. "Do you want to call your mom again and check on Andrew?"

"I'm not that neurotic. I just called her two hours ago," she said wryly.

"Actually, you called her twice in the last hour, but who's counting?"

Karen tried to pull her hand back, so she could cross her arms again.

"I'm teasing." He smiled before turning his head back to the freeway.

"Okay, maybe I'm a little bit neurotic," she admitted.

"Hey, one of those calls I suggested," he reminded her.

She smiled. That made her feel better. Everything about this trip was making her feel pretty damn good. Except for being away from Andrew.

Suck it up, Eastman, oops, Avery. Her name was Avery. God, that sounded good. Karen Marie Avery. She rubbed her thumb against Drake's palm. She couldn't wait to get alone with him tonight. Yesterday she'd gotten the all clear from the doctor. Tonight was going to be a big night, that is if he'd ever stop.

"How much further?" she asked.

"Getting impatient?"

"Yes."

Drake's laugh filled the cab of the truck. "We're almost there."

"We passed all the exits for Bakersfield, I think you messed up."

"Karen, I navigate my way through jungles, I think I can handle the interstate." Drake turned on his blinker. Finally, they were going to stop. She just hoped it was going to be a step up from the Motel Eight she saw advertised on the side of the highway.

She watched as the road slid by, and they pulled up to an impressive log cabin. "Where are we?" she asked as she tried to smother a yawn.

"The Cedar Inn. It's a bed and breakfast."

"This looks like a pretty fancy for a bed and breakfast."

"You deserve fancy."

Karen started to open her door. "Stay there, let me help you out." She smiled. He always insisted on doing that even when they first met. She really liked that.

When the door opened, she noticed how cool the air was. At long last she started to think that it was winter. It had to be forty degrees out, which was nice considering it was seventy degrees when they left San Diego. Seriously, was she never going to experience a winter again?

Drake lifted her out of the truck, their bodies sliding against one another. Oh, it was going to be a good night. "I'll just bring in our overnight bags, we'll unpack for real when we hit Yosemite tomorrow night, how does that sound?" he asked.

"Perfect." She'd put a slinky nightie in her overnight bag. It was going to knock his socks off.

He led her into the reception area and they checked in. Soon they were in their room. It was gorgeous.

"I'm going to take a quick shower and shave," Drake said.

"That's great, it'll give me a chance to change into something more comfortable."

He left the door open a bit when he went into the bathroom. Karen liked that. She loved hearing him doing mundane things. She would never tell him, but she didn't like it when he wasn't home, so when he was around, she savored every second.

This time she was smart and did a quick breast pump, then slipped into the blue nightie and got under the covers. Drake started humming. Another thing that brought her comfort. He always did that when he shaved. She could just picture Drake teaching Andrew to shave, and both of them at the sink, humming together.

SHE LOOKED beautiful sleeping on the soft white sheets. Drake got into bed beside her and she didn't move. The woman was on the go twenty-four/seven with Andrew, and it was no wonder she was asleep. But he couldn't help himself, he had to try. He gathered her into his arms. She shifted, then melted against him, her breathing soft and even. Nope, she hadn't even come close to waking up.

"Dude, you're so not getting any," he said glancing down at his cock. Then he grinned. If he told the truth, all of those early morning feedings with Andrew, and secret meetings with Declan and his team had really taken a toll on his sleep schedule too. He pulled Karen's ass closer to his front, until she was positioned just right. It was the perfect combination of heaven and hell that would allow him to have the best dreams known to mankind.

"DRAKE?" she whispered quietly.

He smiled in the dim glow of morning. Karen's hand rested on his chest, her red hair teased his nose, he was enveloped in the scent of honeysuckle. She pressed the softest of kisses against his heart, and he thought it might beat right out of his chest. Her lips trailed more kisses through his chest hair and he heard her breathe in and then sigh.

"Quit playing possum."

"Shhh, I'm trying to sleep."

"You woke up the second I did. You always do," she said in her husky morning voice.

She had a point. Of course if he didn't, he'd make a piss

poor SEAL. He tangled his fingers through the silk of her hair and tugged. He brought her lips to his. Heat exploded between them. It was a dark magic that had only happened in her arms, he would never be able to get enough of this woman. Drake rolled Karen onto her back and thrust his tongue deep, needing to taste, to dominate, to claim. She made a keening sound and he arched backwards.

"No! You didn't hurt me. Goddammit, I'm fine." She pulled hard on his neck and he settled on top of her again. He watched as she smiled in pleasure and he realized she was fine. She was healed. More, he needed more from his woman. He shoved the cups of her gown down, and stared at her breasts. He loved making her excited, and he knew how he could. He rasped his chest against her breasts, and she moaned low and long.

He licked around her nipple, exciting her, she squirmed, and then her long, long legs lifted and curled around his hips. Shit, she wasn't wearing panties. He'd slept naked. He was seconds away from taking her.

"Now," she demanded. "It's been so long. Now," her husky cry reverberated through the room.

He pushed the covers away from them and kneeled. He pulled the nightie over her head. "You're not listening," her voice quivered with need.

He couldn't find words. He was about to make love to his wife for the first time, words were beyond him. He molded her flesh, rejoicing in the sight of his dark hands claiming her pale skin. She was his. She would always be his. She arched into his touch, and when his fingers found her core, she parted her legs, inviting him into to her very core.

Drake had been so careful with her since the birth of their son, he now found himself shuddering as he felt the heat of her sex clenching his fingers. She was going to burn him alive. He coaxed more liquid arousal from her, then brought his hand to his mouth so he could taste. She watched him with avid eyes.

"You're so bad," she breathed.

"You like bad."

"Yes, I do," she hissed as he parted her legs further, then settled between them. He was going to feast.

"No, enough foreplay. Sex now."

Drake laughed. Seemed his redhead was getting angry. He parted her folds, and swiped his tongue through her drenched flesh. She shrieked softly but it wasn't in anger. He lapped up her honey and that excited him as much as it did her. It had been so long since they had been together, he wanted to make sure she was ready for him, so he tested her depths. Again, and again, he plied her with his fingers, loving the sounds she made as he found the perfect spot as he readied her for their joining.

"Now."

He grinned in the morning light as he licked her swollen bud.

"Please, take me," she gasped.

Not before she went up in flames. He stroked and swirled. She arched and moaned.

"Drake, oh my God. Yes."

She bucked up against him and then he felt her shatter. He couldn't wait another second. He had to be connected to his wife. Quickly, he sheathed himself in a condom, then liquid fire surrounded him as he melded his body to Karen's. Her gleaming green eyes shone brightly.

"So good. I've needed this so much, Drake. It's so good."

Her foot trailed up the back of his leg and pressed into his ass. She was trying to force him to go faster. Deeper.

Well, his wife was just going to have to wait, they were doing things on his terms.

She bit his neck, and he lost it, plunging deeper. Molten fire enveloped him. His head was going to explode. She scraped her teeth against his neck, and clenched her internal muscles.

"God, Karen, what are you doing?" he groaned.

"I'm loving you."

"You're driving me fucking crazy."

"Good," she purred. "Now fucking move."

He didn't have a choice.

He pulled out, her body felt sublime, the clasp of her body tried to keep him, and he pushed back in. Again, and again, a deep and powerful rhythm emerged. It had never been like this before. Her green eyes glittered, but it was as if he saw all the way into her heart. No not that, even deeper, into her soul. The pleasure he was feeling was a connection that could only be felt when two halves of a whole finally found one another. That was his last conscious thought before rapture exploded through his being.

James Eastman - A Week Later

He stared down at the envelope that had arrived special delivery and he slit it open with his pocket knife. He picked up the first newspaper clipping, it was from the London Evening Standard. It gave a succinct account of a sheikh with suspected ties to ISIS who had been found dead aboard his yacht four miles off the coast of Qatar. What made this situation particularly humiliating was pictures had made their way to the web of him having been engaged in autoerotic asphyxia while surrounded by gay pornography. The London paper went on to say that the sheikh's father was insisting that this was a set-up perpetrated by enemies of his son. The story stated that if it were in fact retribution for something, that it had been perfectly executed to shake up members of the Arab community since homosexuality is punishable by death in their religion.

THE SECOND PIECE of paper wasn't a newspaper clipping, it was a one-page printout from an internet site. It explained how the Lius, a Chinese family thought to control one of the most ruthless gangs in all of Shanghai, recently lost billions in a newly created cryptocurrency called Shi-Coin. They had been duped into believing they were in on the ground floor of a Chinese government backed competitor to Bitcoin. Further they had been convinced that the Asian leaders would soon outlaw the Western payment system and Shi-Coin's stock would skyrocket. When the family lost almost every penny, the patriarch, Zhang Liu brought his two sons to his home and shot them before turning the gun on himself.

AN ARTICLE from the Arizona Republic Newspaper was the third piece in the envelope. It stated that Kevin Decault, the wealthy rancher who had been missing for over a week was found last night by a ranch hand. The body was naked, bound to a fencepost, wrapped in barbed wire, in a frozen back pasture of his ranch. He was surrounded by four of his prize-winning bulls. According to the county coroner, he had bled out due to multiple puncture wounds inflicted by the horns of the animals.

JAMES HEARD Wilma in the hallway, just before she knocked on the doorjamb of his study he slipped the papers back into the envelope but left out the picture, then pushed away from his desk, making room for his wife. She walked in and smiled, then kissed the top of his head and slipped onto his lap.

He watched his wife's delicate fingers trace the smiling faces of Drake and Karen, then rested on their grandson. They were enjoying the San Diego beach. Drake was wearing a wet-suit and Karen was gorgeous in a green summer dress, her smile absolutely blinding. James had never seen his daughter look so happy. Four-month-old Andrew Mason's features had filled out, and he was a perfect blending of his parents. He had his mother's eyes and smile, but James knew that everything else would be all Avery.

"They look happy," Wilma said.

"Even better, they're safe," James said with satisfaction.

"I couldn't ask for anything more than safe and happy. Except maybe for my husband to come to bed with me." Wilma smiled.

"You don't have to ask me twice." James kissed the love of his life, content in the knowledge that Drake Avery had kept his promise.

THE END

ABOUT THE AUTHOR

Caitlyn O'Leary is an avid reader and considers herself a fan first and an author second. She reads a wide variety of genres but finds herself going back to happily-ever-afters. Getting a chance to write, after years in corporate America, is a dream come true. She hopes her stories provide the kind of entertainment and escape she has found from some of her favorite authors.

As of winter 2018 she has fourteen books in her two best-selling Navy SEAL series; Midnight Delta and Black Dawn. What makes them special is their bond to one another, and the women they come to love.

She also writes a Paranormal series called the Found. It's been called a Military / Sci-Fi / Action-Adventure thrill ride. The characters have special abilities, that make them targets.

The books that launched her career, is a steamy and loving menage series called Fate Harbor. It focuses on a tight knit community in Fate Harbor Washington, who live, love and care for one another.

Her other two series are The Sisters and the Shadow Alliance. You will be seeing more for these series in 2018.

Keep up with Caitlyn O'Leary:

Facebook: tinyurl.com/nuhvey2
Twitter: @CaitlynOLearyNA
Pinterest: tinyurl.com/q36uohc
Goodreads: tinyurl.com/nqy66h7
Website: www.caitlynoleary.com
Email: caitlyn@caitlynoleary.com
Newsletter: http://bit.ly/1WIhRup
Instagram: http://bit.ly/29WaNIh

ALSO BY CAITLYN O'LEARY

Made in the USA
Las Vegas, NV
13 December 2023